The Hidden Truth always c
Steve took out his phor
the group, who still hadn't noticed him. "Hey, guys, you got a second?"

They all stared at Steve.

He held up his phone. "I overheard you talking about someone named Becky. She seems like a real slut. Am I right?"

It got a few chuckles from the crowd.

"Anyone want to test a new app for me? It's free right now. We're trying to get content for it. You'd all be a big help," Steve said.

"What do you need from us?"

Steve grinned. "I need you to download the app to your phones and start telling the world what a piece of shit whore Becky is."

THE
HIDDEN TRUTH

ARMAND ROSAMILIA
——— AND ———
JAY WILBURN

CHAPTER 1

Mississippi Gulf Town Trailer Park Ravaged by Redneck Vampires
Warning: Nudity in This Issue

They rolled past the first two burned out doublewides before Jackson Wrath turned off the headlights on his Buick. The bad brakes whistled to announce their stop on the gravel path four dark and ruined trailers later.

Cull Staples stepped out on the passenger's side first, hoisting the bulk of his camera and a tall flash which accounted for half the weight. The support handle on the side had the girth of a metal baseball bat. He had switched from film to digital back before he stopped shooting weddings and switched to crime scenes. Even after twenty years of snapping paranormal and unexplained stories for the tabloid, he still felt leaving film behind was his biggest betrayal.

Jackson pocketed the keys and slammed the driver's door with a crash worthy of a bank vault. A spare ignition key sat under the back edge of the driver's mat. They both knew about it, if it ever came to that.

Cull rounded the front bumper with his camera up and ready. Jackson fell in beside him and unclipped the mini mag light from his belt, but kept it off and lowered to his side because that's how Cull wanted it in these situations.

"You know the joke about vampire stories, right?" Cull lowered to one knee and flashed two pictures like bolts of heat lightning.

Jackson blinked away the spots in his vision. "No, I don't think so. Six or seven years of these road trips and I swore I had heard every story and joke you knew to tell. You must have found a new one between surfing porn sites, I guess."

Cull lowered the camera, but then raised it to snap a third of the same curled aluminum peeling off the side of a trailer like an open wound. The flash revealed the corner of a sofa and crushed cans inside the opening. That damage could have been old, but digital photography and creative editing knew no bounds.

Cull stood and they resumed their stroll. "No, I only go to the site with your mother on it. Stick with what works."

"See, that joke I've heard at least a dozen times. You stick with it, too, even though it doesn't work." Jackson pointed to the left. "How about this shit?"

Cull stopped and squinted. All he saw was a hanging cactus hooked to a porch which had pulled away from the door to the trailer and was tilted at a sickly angle. He almost asked Jackson to ignite his flashlight, but then he saw it too.

He blasted off five bolts of lightning and then walked right up under the thing to take a sixth and seventh shot. Jackson remained on the trail and turned to watch the deeper shadows around them.

Twists of rough bristle like a rustic broom head formed what could have been the arms, legs, and head of a figure within a hoop of wood, twisting from the disembodied porch. "This is classic, man. It's like a throwback to that *Blair Witch* stuff. Readers will be creeped out by this and not know why."

"It's probably a gnarled-up dreamcatcher coming apart in the humidity," Jackson said. "Let's see if we can find something we couldn't fake in the office."

Cull stepped out and they followed the curve of the path by more abandoned and collapsing structures. The metal skirts folded open on most, revealing wheels and webs underneath. He snapped a few wider shots as they walked. "I'm sure we'll fake a few more once we get back. It is soupy tonight, speaking of humidity. I could do without the mosquitos, too. Maybe a real vampire will come along and the mosquitos will leave like in the movies."

"Is that a thing?" Jackson waved his dark flashlight in the

air. "Maybe he'll exude cold off his undead flesh and we'll cool off from ninety degrees and a hundred and five percent humidity at ten o'clock at night."

"Ten o'clock at night." Cull wagged a finger on the hand not holding the camera. "The joke about hunting vampires."

"Good. Can't wait to see how this ends up being about my mother."

Cull grunted a laugh and then said, "In all the vampire movies, the angry villagers hang around deciding what to do about the vampire in the castle until it's dark. Then, they get torches and pitchforks ready to take him on after he wakes up. If you're not dealing with glittery heartthrob vampires, why not hunt them during the day? Stupid to go at night." Cull panned the scene with the lens of his camera without taking a shot. "But here we are. Two stupid villagers."

"Yeah, we got lost. That's why we're here at night."

Cull clicked his tongue. "Well, that and night pictures are creepier."

"We can doctor pictures to make day look like night and to make the shots look creepier," Jackson said. "Better than real life."

"Now there's the hidden truth behind every issue of *Hidden Truth* since the heydays of the roaring eighties," Cull said. "No imagination."

"Shit. In the eighties, I was still in high school and you were still trying to be a legit nature photographer, right? We missed the heydays they're always talking about."

"Yeah, all our greatest failures were still in front of us."

"Did you hear the one about the two guys who decided to split the cost on a high class–"

A piece of sheet metal blew out from the corner of a trailer near the column of a suspended air conditioner unit. Before the piece hit the ground, the shape soared into the air over the trail in front of them.

Cull brought up the camera and fired off blast after blast following the motion without taking time to aim. The deer's hooves connected with the ground and crossed in two bounds. Cull followed it until it vanished around another corner.

"Jesus, good jump scare," Jackson said, "but it'll still look like pictures of a deer. You're back to your dream of nature photography. Congratulations, Cull."

"Thanks, asshole. One of the pics will probably be blurry enough to 'Bigfoot' ourselves a nice vampire."

A porch light flipped on and the door to a trailer a couple lots ahead on the right opened. The hinges crackled and the chain clapped against the top of the door. A heavy woman with unruly, long grey hair in a pink bathrobe emerged at the top of her wooden steps.

"Are you two here about the vampire attacks?"

"If she ends draining us dry with her fangs, this will be exactly how I want my career to end," Cull whispered next to Jackson. He raised his voice to say, "Uh, yes, ma'am. We're with *Hidden Truth Magazine.*"

"Really? I used to read that back in the eighties. Thought you guys went under."

Jackson whispered, "Her eighties or the 1980s?"

"They don't carry you at the Stop-N-Shop anymore. You should call them and tell them you're still around. Especially if you run this vampire story. People around here would read that."

"We'll do that. That's good advice. Thank you." Cull took a step toward her. "Would you mind giving us the story here?"

"Is there money in it?"

Cull shot a glance at Jackson and then rolled them. "Yes, always. As soon as the story runs, they always cut the big checks for all our contributors."

"I only have warm beer on account of my fridge being out again, but you can come on in."

As they walked toward her porch where she held the door, Jackson bowed his head and said, "Is there a joke about two tabloid reporters being invited in by the only old woman in an abandoned trailer park?"

"Yeah, we're the joke, as usual. Last one out alive writes the touching memorial for the other."

Cull sniffed. "That no one will get to read at the Biloxi Stop-N-Shop."

They stepped into the darkness of the trailer and she closed the door behind them, leaving only a harsh shaft from the porch through the square of glass on the door. The room smelled of dirty laundry and wet mold.

She cracked on the switch and the fluorescents flickered up with a struggle.

The sofa, crushed beer cans on the floor, broad stains which flattened and hardened the carpet, the open refrigerator with black spots radiating out from the plastic seals, and, of course, the picture of a forlorn Jesus staring up into a brown and tan sky. This disaster was decorated like a hundred other trailers they had been in before and wasn't out of place with the other husks of homes which made up the abandoned park. Abandoned except for her, of course.

Jackson sidestepped away from the door and the woman. "Why are you still here?"

"You mean with the vampires coming around?" she asked. The top of her robe parted on wrinkles, liver spots, and deep blue veins.

Jackson couldn't make himself look away. "Sure."

"My home is my home. It isn't much, but it's mine. Can't give it up because monsters want to take it. Besides, I think they've mostly moved on to feed other places."

Cull took a picture of the living room sprawl and then sat on the sofa. Dust billowed and sliced through the air and pale light. "You must be quite brave to stand your ground like this. You opened the door and stepped right out when you heard us. We could have been more vampires, you know."

She shrugged and more sagging boob came free. "We're always standing up to something, ain't we? If it isn't the vampires, it's the government."

"You mind if I get a shot of you for the story?" Cull lifted the camera off his knee by its baseball bat handle.

She patted the front of her robe and looked down without closing the breach in the halves of the pink cloth. "I'm not really presentable."

"Doesn't matter," Cull said. "This is a story of a survivor standing her ground against the monsters. You look like you've won a hard-fought victory."

"Are you sure?"

"Absolutely." Jackson looked from her blue veins to Cull. "Your story and your image will help others face these monsters. Vampires don't stop. They'll just hit another innocent trailer park and then another. Probably all along the Gulf."

Cull pointed at Jackson. "That's right. Then, who knows? The rest of the Bible Belt? People have to know and they have to see someone like them who stood up and won. You'd be saving people probably. A real hero."

"Who can be presentable after fighting off the undead like this?" Jackson patted her shoulder.

"Well, I guess."

Cull lifted the camera and she placed her hands on her hips. One hairy thigh showed as the robe parted farther in her stance. The flash strobed as Cull knocked off a set of pictures.

"We'll need you to sign a release before we go, so we can run these great photos of you," Jackson said. He glanced at forlorn Jesus averting his eyes to the dusty sky. It seemed to Jackson the perfect answer to *What Would Jesus Do* in a situation like this.

"Of course." She spoke through clenched teeth as she held her crooked smile for Cull.

Cull lowered the camera. "Those were great."

"Tell us what happened here," Jackson said.

He sat on the couch next to Cull as she began. "They came down out of the sky. They went after the younger ones first. The children and the pretty girls in their cutoffs so high up their asses that the pockets showed out from the bottom and the bikini tops instead of shirts."

"You're still here," Cull said. "They missed at least one of the pretty girls."

"Stop." Her belt slipped the knot and Jackson saw she had a least one C-section below the fold of her belly. She hadn't shaved her legs, but it looked like she took the time to shave elsewhere. "Some of the men tried to fight them the first few nights, but they didn't do well. The police didn't believe us and the families that were left tried to run for it. Some of them made it, but not all."

"What did they look like?" Cull adjusted the angle of his flash.

"Hairy. Most had beards. Big and burly. Couple of them wore camo and hunter orange. Baseball caps too. Mostly Braves caps. They had fangs, too, of course. I'm thinking they may have been mostly locals what got turned and formed their own coven here, you know? Real good ole boys turned vampire, is what I'm saying."

"What are police saying about the disappearances then?" Jackson asked.

Cull snapped a few more pictures of her open robe. She clutched it closed in the middle, but didn't cover the parts she might have meant to. Her nipples were two different shades of brown. "They don't believe it. Or they're covering it up to avoid the bad press."

"Good thing we're here to tell your story," Jackson said.

"And the check." Cull snapped another picture. "Don't forget the big check when the story runs."

"Right. That too." Jackson scratched his nose. When he placed his hand on the arm of the sofa, it felt greasy, so he pulled it back to his knee. "Maybe the police are in on it, you know? Like working with the vampires or covering for them for some reason."

"I hadn't considered that." She lost her grip on her robe. "How big of a check are we talking about? I have a lot of repairs around here on account of the vampire attacks."

"Right. Well, that depends."

She stared at Cull with her hands on her hips. "Depends on how good my story is?"

"And how explicit the pictures are that we come back with." Cull waved at her and then the door to the trailer. "The damage. The evidence of the attacks. The mystery. And the witnesses. It's a modern audience, looking for edgy material."

"And you guys are losing readership what with the Internet and the Stop-N-Shops dropping you, right?"

Cull cleared his throat. "That's right. Explicit or gory are our bread and butter. If it bleeds, it leads. If it horrifies, the money flies. If we see the stuff, the check is enough. That might as well be the letterhead at *The Hidden Truth*."

"You guys still pay for the nudie bits in between the stories then?" She opened her robe. "Started that in the nineties when people stopped reading so much. I remember that. Maybe that's why the Stop-N-Shop didn't carry you anymore."

"It works for the online version of the issues." Cull lifted the camera and she held her hips without protest.

"Is standing here good?"

Cull took his pictures in deliberate flashes with pauses between.

"Do you want me to keep telling about the vampires then?"

"Of course." The back of the camera muffled Cull's voice. "That's why we're here."

"One of them got this twenty-year-old with fake boobs down on the ground and started tearing at her clothes. Others dropped on her and started draining her from every side and every tender spot you can image. There were others still around. Humans, I mean. They just watched it happen. They watched them do that to her. She fought and screamed at first, but then, I think she was starting to like it." Her fingers went to her nipples down near her deep navel and she stared through the wall above their heads.

"That's great," Cull said. "Keep going. Can you turn for me while you talk, Dear? Yeah, that's good."

Jackson scraped his tongue along his teeth and the roof of his mouth, but couldn't seem to clear a greasy film which reminded him of the arm of the couch. He shook his head and stared down at the mini mag still in his hands and never turned on.

"You guys want one of those beers? They're warm on account of my fridge breaking though. How soon did you say that check would come?"

"Soon. Soon. Do you want a beer, Jackson?"

"I'll pass for now. Don't want to break up this great story." He saw her toes and hairy shins over the flashlight as she finished her turn for Cull's camera. One of her toenails was black and ready to fall off. Another was polished purple with red glitter, but it was the only one adorned at all. "Probably frontpage stuff, don't you think, Cull?"

"You know, a story like this? I bet it will be. That's a big payout."

"Okay, well, she was on the ground then … naked … and all of them was on her, like I said …."

"Oh." Jackson leaned forward by Cull's ear as the lady continued her story. "Don't forget to get her name before we go."

CHAPTER 2

Biloxi Seafood Eatery Turning Tourists into Zombies

"Stop taking pictures so I can order some food," Jackson said and shook his head.

"Why? This is some creepy shit in this place." Cull snapped two more shots of the giant plastic squid on the wall. "Remember the monster octopus story we were working on? I bet I can play with these pictures enough to scare a few readers."

"An octopus and a squid are two different things. Don't make the bull mistake again," Jackson said and waved at the waitress, who seemed more interested in staring at her fingernails than helping an actual customer.

"A bull is a male cow. It's like calling a rooster a hen. You screwed up by using the wrong picture," Jackson said. He put up his hand before Cull could argue, the same pointless argument again. "You were wrong. Admit it."

"The cow was possessed by an alien lifeform. Maybe if your article had been a little clearer, you could've mentioned it also turned the sex of the cattle, too." Cull smiled at the waitress, who finally came over to take their orders. "We'll have the seafood combo and a round of beers. By round I mean we each want three to start."

Jackson held up one finger. "A single beer would be fine for me. Can you smoke in here?"

She looked confused before shaking her head.

Cull took a picture of her ass as she walked away. He grinned. "This will be for personal use back at the hotel."

"Gross. Especially since we're sharing a room." Jackson

wanted a smoke. He needed one after tonight. This was going to be another vampire story like the last five they'd done. He knew they always sold, but he wanted something more. Something with real journalistic integrity behind it. "I hope you know I'm not paying for a seafood combo. I'm down to my last twenty." Cull waved his hand. "Relax. I'll get it and turn it in as soon as we get back. Once we finish this piece, we can go back to the octopus/squid god living under the ocean story. I think it has legs." He grinned. "Get it, legs? Because they don't have legs. They have those things…"

Now Jackson wished he'd gone with his first instinct and not said a word to the waitress about only one beer. He didn't think he'd get through this night sober. "I need to take a few drags. Let me know when the beer arrives. If it ever does."

The waitress was back in her usual spot looking at her nails.

"You really only got a twenty on you?" Cull asked.

"It might be a ten and some singles. Why?"

Cull shrugged. "We're in Biloxi. There's a casino or ten right down the road. Maybe we go and see if Lady Luck wants to spread her legs for us tonight."

"I've seen enough hairy legs for one night." Jackson made sure he lit his cigarette the second he got outside. He inhaled deeply, blowing smoke at the Moon. Mississippi was nice. As nice as anywhere else in the South that was hot all the time, even at night. At least he had a nice breeze off the bay.

His phone rang and he took another drag. It was too late at night for phone calls that were good. The restaurant would be closing soon. He needed his beer and some food before sleep. It would be a long, boring ride east on I-10 at first light.

It rang again.

"Yeah?" Jackson knew the number. It was Marty, their editor. Nothing good *ever* happened when Marty called after five, when his work day ended. This was going to be bad.

"We got a problem, Cull," Marty said.

You little motherfucker, Jackson thought. "This is Jackson. The one who actually writes this shit."

Marty chuckled. The guy was a super sleazy bastard who always wanted more from them. Sexier or more horrific pictures.

More over the top cliché horror in the writeup. If you looked in the dictionary for tabloid editor, Marty Carroll would light up the page. "I know which number I called. Just having some fun at your expense."

"This can't be anything too bad if you're joking with me this late at night."

Marty was suddenly silent on the other end.

Jackson sighed loudly. He paced and took another drag off his cigarette. Despite the slight breeze off the water, he was sweating. He wiped his forehead with the back of the hand holding the smoke.

A happy couple, hand-in-hand, strolled past and into the restaurant. Jackson hated them. Hated their happiness and their love and the fact they were together and they'd have crazy tourist sex in an expensive casino hotel room tonight while he was stuck listening to Cull masturbate to the pictures of asses he'd taken over the years.

"Uh…no reaction?" Marty asked.

Jackson closed his eyes. "What did you say? I was thinking about this article. It's going to be amazing. Trust me."

"I said the paper had to put another round of cuts together. I'm sorry."

Jackson opened his eyes and made a fist, crushing his cigarette in his fingers. "Wait…what are you talking about?"

"Budget cuts. *The Hidden Truth* is bleeding money. Lots of money. They needed to cut another few people," Marty said.

"How many others lost their jobs tonight?"

Another pause from Marty.

"Goddamnit, tell me the truth, Marty. I've been putting up with your shit for a long time. You fucking owe me that," Jackson said. He was pacing furiously now, nearly barreling over another happy couple leaving the bar. "How many?"

"Just you and Cull. I thought I was calling him. I wanted him to tell you."

"Lying Chicken-shit. You knew I'd be pissed. You'd be able to smooth it out with Cull. Give him some bullshit lies about eventually coming back or freelancing his work. Lies. All lies. Do we even get a severance package?"

"No. As of midnight tonight you're both unemployed. Good luck out there. It's rough for anything but Internet garbage now. Everyone's doing what we're doing on their Facebook page for free. The kids have ruined the media," Marty said.

"Then, that's it for us? There's not another job we could do until the economy changes or someone buys the paper?" Jackson asked, knowing he was grasping at straws.

Some people lived paycheck to paycheck. He lived day to day with his money, never knowing if he'd have enough gas money or be able to afford another pack of cigarettes. As it was, he smoked the cheapest ones he could find.

"I'm sorry. To be honest, The Hidden Truth might have six more months to crawl before it's ancient history. I'm sure I'll be gone soon, too," Marty said.

"Without us, who are you going to rely on? The kids can't handle the big stories. None of them have gone into the field and done actual research. They just spell-check my shit and make sure the pictures go with the right story," Jackson said. He pulled another cigarette from his pack. Now he really wished he'd ordered three beers. Cull was probably already into his sixth or seventh, thinking he was going to have a good night.

"We have enough in the archive to push us through another few months. I overheard management talking about paying one of those shitty half-penny-a-word places to write generic articles to use. If you want, I'll find out where they'll be sourcing them from and put in a good word for you," Marty said. "I know you think I'm an asshole."

"It's never been a secret."

"As much as we bumped heads, I knew you were one of the best I've ever worked with. When we switched to only bullshit articles, you never fussed. You never threw your weight around. You just did your fucking job, Jackson. I won't ever forget it," Marty said.

Jackson knew there was some truth in what he said, even though it was tossed out there to calm Jackson so he wouldn't explode. Marty didn't like confrontation. He'd rather smooth it out. He'd missed his calling as a politician.

"Your nice words and a buck get me a cup of coffee," Jackson said.

"More like two bucks...I mean, yeah...sorry again. You can grab your shit tomorrow when you return," Marty said. "I'll do my best to get your trip paid for, too."

"Great. They'll screw us out of all this hotel and gas money. Cull just ordered the seafood special."

"I'd see if you can stretch it over a few meals," Marty said. From the sound of his voice, Jackson knew he was trying to be helpful.

"I'm really screwed," Jackson said, more to himself.

"I promise to give a great reference. Let Cull know, too. You'll land on your feet. You might not be young, but you have experience. Maybe one of these online websites will hire you. They have all those fancy spinning ads and apps and videos," Marty said.

Jackson stopped pacing and took the cigarette from his mouth. "Wait...stop."

"Sorry," Marty said softly, misinterpreting Jackson.

"We'll be back in town by the time the boss gets in. I know how we're not only going to save our jobs but also save *The Hidden Truth* from closing," Jackson said. He started heading back into the restaurant.

"How?"

Jackson laughed. Was it that simple? "I've been kicking around an idea for an app. It would be cheap to put together and the beauty is the readers would feed it news stories. I'll see you in the morning. Have a pot of coffee ready, Marty."

CHAPTER 3

Chinese Hookers Steal Black Market Kidneys from Gamblers Up and Down the Mississippi

"Are you fucking kidding me right now?"

"They said they'd give us a ride back to our hotel," Cull said as he leaned on the wall outside the doors to the casino. His head hung down almost to the point of being upside down. He stood on the edge of the decorative landscaping where the light met darkness. Smoke from his cigarette floated up along that edge of floodlight beams. "Apparently, people gamble away their cars all the time."

Jackson balled his fists and used every bit of restraint he had left to keep himself from punching Cull in the ear while he wasn't looking. "It wasn't your car to gamble away, Dumb Ass. And what damn difference does it make if we get a ride back to our motel, if we have no way to get back home when we check out in the morning?"

"We don't have jobs, remember? What are we going back home to?"

Jackson rubbed his face with both hands and turned away from Cull. "To hell with you, Cull. I'm not going to circle the damn drain with you anymore."

"You can tell them it wasn't my car. They'll take it out on me and you can get the car back. I'll find my own bail and my own way back after that."

"Jesus, Cull, this isn't a damn mobster movie. You aren't going to work your debt off with the bosses. Life isn't one of our stupid made up articles. You fucked us over and you can't unfuck it by just being sorry and miserable. Why didn't you gamble away your camera instead of my car?"

"You know the answer to that."

"Yeah, you're a selfish asshole."

"What do you want to do then, Jackson? We're going to come swooping back into the place that fired us with a little computer phone game and get us raises instead of pink slips? Is that the master plan now? How long have you been working on that thing? Forever last Tuesday?"

"Go straight to Hell, Cull. Drag yourself down. Sit in the gutter. Find your next ex-wife in another Mississippi dive and never crawl out again. I'm tired of rolling down this hill with you."

"Oh, that's rich, Jackson. Sorry, I've been holding you back all these years." Cull lifted his head and took a long drag off the cigarette. Smoke puffed out with each syllable after that. "Sorry I landed you in jail right after you picked up your diploma before we met. Sorry about fucking up a research job so bad you got yourself and your whole team fired from your last real journalism job. You know, before we met. Sorry about you knocking around for years on conspiracy websites. And I'm really, really sorry about being your partner all these years we hung on to these jobs. I'm sure you would have made a real name for yourself in the tabloid business without me. Now you can spread your wings, my beautiful butterfly, and show me how you're going to fly free without me in your way."

Jackson spit on the sidewalk and stepped toward the parking lot. "You gambled away all your money and my car too, Cull. What the hell is wrong with you?"

"I'm sorry about that, too," Cull spoke at Jackson's retreating back. "Listen, I might be able to get some bus tickets back to Jacksonville and we can pick up a ride from someone to Flagler Beach after that. We'll present your idea to Marty and the boss and see what happens."

"Take care of your own ticket then. I'll either see you or I won't."

Jackson took out his phone and scrolled through the rideshare apps. Uber …Lyft …CurbSyde….

He thumbed one and put in the request for the next town over. Middle of the night. Trying to hop rides all the way along I-10 to Florida. What a nightmare!

"My whole life...."

His e-mail still had backed up requests for fixes to the magazine's website. Unbelievable. Even with being on the road and now being fired, they still expected him to bumble through the I.T. issues since they fired the guy who knew what he was doing.

Jackson pulled up his Carbonite account and panicked when he saw it was inactive. He rolled his eyes and remembered he had switched to a cheaper service once *The Hidden Truth* stopped paying for it.

He opened the new backup and the files for The Hidden Truth app. Sort of a file share. Sort of a crowdsource. Sort of a social media with a tiered pay platform option. Sort of genius. Sort of insane. If he could get it to work though....

A notification popped up and he swiped away from his files and unfinished code. Steve Chance was coming in a white Honda Accord to pick him up for the first leg of his journey.

Jackson shut off his phone and walked through the sprawling casino parking lot to the street. Somewhere in here was his car. The spare key from under the mat was inside with one of the managers. Jackson felt pretty sure the title was in a file box at his loft over a deli in Flagler Beach. Maybe he should hang Cull out to dry and get his car back for whatever it was worth.

Cull could hang for a decade and never dry out.

Jackson stood on the street without seeing a car pass for several minutes. He thought about showing up at the offices without a shower, stinking of day-old seafood platter, cigarettes, and road stink. Then what? A PowerPoint presentation on a half-finished app?

"What the hell am I doing?" It wasn't the first time he had asked it out loud, alone or with company. The empty highway had no answer for him.

His phone buzzed in his pocket and he opened it to a message from the rideshare app: *I'm here in the parking lot. The guy I asked at the door said Jackson Wrath could go f*** himself. Are you nearby, I assume?*

Jackson laughed despite the situation. He typed: *Out at the end of the lot by the highway. Near the main sign. I thought I was making it easier. Sorry.*

On the way, Steve Chance in the white Honda typed.

He pulled up and Jackson stepped in the back.

Steve wore a ballcap and looked like he had just graduated high school. He still had his whole life to screw up. Jackson wasn't sure if he envied the boy or pitied him.

"Glad you are working the nightshift, Steve."

"Sure thing. Casinos make for good work at this sort of job for those who can still see the buttons on their phone."

"I'll bet. You mind if we swing by my hotel to collect a bag before we hit the road?"

"It works for me. Which one is it?" They pulled out of the parking lot and made a right. Jackson wasn't sure that was the correct direction. He wasn't sure he cared either.

"Ugh, Econo … something. It's by the seafood place on the bay. The one with the cartoon crab on the sign?"

"The Giant Crab Buffet?"

"It wasn't a buffet."

"That doesn't narrow it down much. I know what road you mean though. If I drove past it, you think you'd recognize it enough to give me the high sign."

"Yeah, I can do that."

Steve made another right on a red light at an empty intersection. "Did you know that guy outside the casino or does he just hate you on general principle?"

"He's been my partner at the magazine for several years. He just gambled away my car and I have to get back to Jacksonville in a last-ditch effort to save my job."

Steve adjusted his rearview mirror. "Jacksonville, Florida? Holy smokes, man. Are you going to ride hop on the app all the way to Florida? You should probably look at a bus or a plane ticket."

"Yeah, I should probably do a lot of things. If you want to take me the whole way, I can split the cost up over five or six credit cards, I think."

Steve made another right at a stop sign. "Yeah, I think I'll pass. Just caught my girlfriend cheating on me with one of my old high school teachers who lives three doors down from my parents. Apparently, the whole town knew about it before I did. Had a job and an internship fall through, so I'll be giving rides to guys from the casino with bad friends for the foreseeable future."

"So, what's stopping you from leaving this shitstorm behind for Florida beaches?"

Steve made a left and stopped at the red light for another empty intersection. Houses stood dark on both sides of them. A dog barked from the darkness behind a chain link fence.

"Because every town is full of the same bullshit. I don't have to drive all night to figure that out."

"You're driving back and forth all night anyway," Jackson said. "Your asshole high school teacher and shitty ex-girlfriend aren't in Flagler Beach though."

"Thought you said Jacksonville."

"Yes, they're within an hour. *The Hidden Truth* offices are in Flagler. The publishing office, I mean. It's owned by a media conglomerate. They have a bigger office in Jacksonville and New York and in…. Doesn't matter. They're the same place basically."

"The tabloid?" Is that who you work for…worked for?"

The light turned green.

"I think I can pull it out, if I can present the app idea and get it working."

Steve rolled through the intersection, leaving the barking dog behind. "What app?"

"I want to move the magazine and reporting online. It'll be a sort of multi-tiered system where people report stories, reporters and tech work to verify, and we give people in the stories a chance to comment or to confirm or deny."

Steve followed a curve of service road which sounded like gravel and sand under the wheels until they merged onto the Bay Road which Jackson recognized from earlier.

"Let me know when you see the right Econo-whatever."

Jackson leaned forward in the seat. "It'll be on the water side a little farther down."

"Is the app going to collect the same alien anal probe and monsters attack kind of stories?"

Jackson clicked his tongue and sighed. "That and the true crime stuff, too, I think. People still eat that stuff up. If we had an endless supply of those stories from everywhere, I think people would be all over it and be itching to tell their own. I think we could float the paper on the ads alone not to mention the premium pay tiers."

"People are going to snitch on each other then?"

"Where do you think we get those stories now, man?"

"I used to study programming. I even did a few apps for my degree program. One was an exercise and goals app. It's nothing big, but I still get a few residuals from it."

"I think it's the one after this light. Next to the seafood place." Jackson cleared his throat.

"That's the Economy Stay Lodge next to the Crabadashery Diner. Good choice in food, but with that motel, you might want to just burn your suitcases on the sidewalk and start over."

"That's kind of what I'm doing with my life most days." They stopped at the light within view of the darkened diner where he shared what might have been his last meal with Cull. The angry red vacancy sign of their motel greeted him. He tried to remember what room his key went to.

It was an actual key and not a magnetic card. *What did they do if someone walked off with the key? Or waited with it for the next person to check in? That might be a story to make readers tingle.*

Jackson said, "Would you know how to create the kind of system I'm talking about, if I gave you the base files and some of the coding?"

"Probably." Steve drummed his fingers on the steering wheel. A blue sedan passed them on the right and ran the light without a pause. Steve waited on it to turn. "If I was great, I'd probably have either the shitty job or the really great unpaid internship right now instead of driving you one town closer to a beach in Florida."

"You could drive me closer than that and we could work on this thing together."

The light turned green and Steve rolled on. "I could program an app from here and save myself the drive."

He eased into the turn lane and used his signal before

pulling into the motel parking lot. He killed his lights and parked in a spot on the middle island of weeds.

"You could also drive somewhere that you didn't have to see your girl and your high school teacher playing tongue tag from your parents' driveway."

"Hey, easy, man. I just found that out today. It's a bit raw."

"Yet, you told me right after we met. You want to drive in circles for sad sacks like me or you want to come help me present an idea that can save an American institution?"

Steve snorted and shook his head. "*The Hidden Truth*? I don't know about an American institution."

"You can always drive yourself right back, if things don't go the way you like. Worst case, you have a couple days in Florida and you're back here in time for the next weekend rush at the casino."

"Worst case is probably more along the lines of you murdering me in the woods somewhere near the Alabama line."

Jackson laughed. "Okay, you really do need to come work for *The Hidden Truth*."

"Sounds like you and your best frenemy back at the casino barely work there now."

"That's true. This is all a long shot. I have to get back though, and I have to try. Someone is going to help me do it. Thought this might be one of those destiny moments where we could tell this story around expensive tables in New York and Vegas, toasting our success. It would be our 'million-dollar idea from out of a garage' story."

Steve said, "Except your garage has no car in it anymore."

Jackson opened his door, switching on the overhead light. "That's true. I'll get my suitcases and we'll go one town closer before we part ways in the night."

He closed the door and searched for the key as he tried to pinpoint which block of the motel felt familiar. The car engine idled quietly behind him.

Steve called from the driver's window. "Okay, I'll go. I'll need to swing by my folks' place and pack a few things real quick, but then I'll go back with you. I'm still charging you the fare though, in case this all turns out to be bullshit."

Jackson snapped his fingers and turned around. "I'm not going to jinx this by saying you won't regret it, but I'm glad you're coming."

"Because you have no car, you mean?"

"That too."

Jackson turned in the direction of what he decided was his room. He stopped and faced the car again. "You mind if we pick up my buddy Cull before we go by your place? He's probably somewhere between the casino and the bus station. Actually, I'm guessing he's back in the casino."

"As long as you two don't murder me or worse."

Jackson gave a thumbs-up and twirled the key and ring on his finger. He realized the number to his room was printed on there, so he changed course for the other end of the motel. "If anything, Cull and I will kill each other."

CHAPTER 4

The Moon Landing Was Faked by Aliens!

Cull kept his mouth shut until they crossed into Tallahassee. He wanted to ask Jackson why he hadn't left him in Biloxi. It would make sense.

I would've left me if given the choice, he thought. "I need a smoke. Also, a very large drink."

"We have a meeting in a few hours. I need you sober," Jackson said and looked over his shoulder. "As close to sober as you can manage, anyway."

"Your friend smells," Steve said.

"He also has ears, you little runt." Cull leaned against the window and watched darkness fly by. He was sure in the light it wouldn't look any nicer. Trees and chain restaurants littered the landscape. Where were the picturesque little towns in-between? All gone. Covered over by so-called progress and a younger generation who didn't believe in history more than five minutes ago. A generation that had relegated a dinosaur like Cull to the also-rans and never-was section of the Internet.

"You really think this thing of yours will work?" Cull asked, more out of boredom than anything else. It was also nice Jackson was finally coming around and talking to him again.

"I really do," Jackson said. "Once it's launched, it will go viral. I'm sure of it. People like to hear themselves talk. Facebook and Twitter are filled with self-obsessed people who want the world to know what they think. They don't care about anyone else. They'll give us the bulk of the content. The rest will be padded with some of our own stories. Shit, *The Hidden Truth* has a backlist of so many of our stories. They can simply recycle them over and over. People aren't going to remember a story, especially if we change a few facts."

"If it's an app you won't need my pictures," Cull said. He wanted to ask why Jackson had come back for him, especially after the shitty move of losing his car.

"I'll need your photos. The app will be multimedia. We'll have not only articles but your photos as well as video. Some people also like to see and hear themselves talk. The app can do that, too," Jackson said.

Steve snapped his fingers. "People love video. You could also repurpose some of the photos into video, too. Have them move around on the page while the article is being read. People hate having to read shit these days. Trust me. I'd rather be watching it like TV. That's why podcasts are so big right now."

"What's a podcast?" Cull asked and felt old for asking.

"The future, man," Steve said. He tapped his fingers on the steering wheel. "But this app could be the *real* future. It wouldn't take much to get it up and running, either. All it amounts to is time for me. I can build it to your specs. Let it do what you want it to do, but there's so much untapped potential as well. Just thinking about the rss applications is exciting."

Cull didn't know what rss applications meant and didn't bother to ask. He was just happy to be along for the ride. Both figuratively and literally.

"I need something to eat soon," Cull said. He needed to change the subject for a bit because his head was swimming. He also really just needed another drink. This was all moving so fast. One minute he was pounding beers and eating way too much seafood. Then, Jackson had told him the news about being fired, but he had some vague plan about getting their jobs back. Followed by the casino bad luck run. Being left behind by Jackson.

"We're almost home. A few more hours. Once this is pitched, we'll be dining like kings," Jackson said. "We need to keep moving."

"I need to stop for gas," Steve said.

Jackson sighed. "Then we find an exit with gas and food in the middle of the night."

Cull closed his eyes. He was coming down off the highs and lows today. A few months from sixty, but he felt like eighty. The drinking and the bad eating were going to put him in an early grave, although he counted his lucky stars he'd made it this far without a lot of ailments except the stress of the job.

"I think we need to find a diner to sit down and talk before I go any further," Steve said.

"We're in Florida. No such thing as a diner. There might be a truck stop or a Denny's, but that's about it." Jackson rolled down his window. "Maybe you can wash up, Cull? You really do stink."

"That's mean to say." Cull lifted his arm and took a whiff. He did smell. They'd gone from the trailer park to dinner to the casino to the car. He hadn't had time to take a shower.

"The truth hurts," Jackson said.

"You mean the hidden truth?" Steve said and laughed. "We're gonna be rich. Successful. That bitch will know what real pain is. I can't wait to return to Biloxi in a limo. With a pocketful of hundreds."

"Relax, buddy. None of this is settled just yet. As much as Jackson wants to pretend it's a sure bet, there are quite a few hurdles to jump through. You haven't faced 'The Boss' yet." Cull smelled his other armpit and grimaced. It was even worse. "I need a stick of deodorant when we stop."

No one else in the car disagreed.

They drove in silence for many miles, all lost in their own thoughts. Cull was trying to stay positive, but there were too many variables to this plan. Who said Marty or The Boss would even agree to any of this? What if that rat bastard stole the app idea? What if Jackson cut everyone else out?

Cull had spent his life getting his hopes up. Get rich quick schemes had peppered his past. He'd lost more money than he cared to remember on wine, women, and song. Not to mention the gambling problem.

The drinking problem. The drug problem. Every vice imaginable.

Cull looked back on a past littered with broken dreams and broken promises. More women than he cared to remember. Too many he couldn't remember.

The only constant was his trusty camera and skill to use it. It had gotten him by. Kept him as grounded as he'd ever be. He'd slept in his car for weeks many years ago because he couldn't afford a place to crash or gas to drive. He'd kept his camera and drank water from a suspect river and eaten berries that turned his fingers blue as well as his lips. The diarrhea had been sudden and fierce.

"You coming, Cull?" Jackson asked, standing beside the vehicle.

While Cull was looking back at his past, they'd pulled into a gas station with a Subway restaurant attached.

Cull shook the cobwebs loose and got out of the car. Stretching and taking in the parking lot and the big rigs, some coming, some going, others parked for the next few hours, he didn't have any new answers.

Everyone in a hurry to get somewhere else.

"Can I get a six inch and a Coke?" Jackson asked Steve.

Cull sat down at the nearest table as they entered, slapping the table with his palms. "I'll take the same."

"You guys can order whatever you want with your money," Steve said, frowning. "You don't have any money to pay me for the ride or gas, do you?"

Jackson put his hands in the air. "I already explained everything to you. By this time tomorrow, you'll be sleeping in a nice hotel room *The Hidden Truth* is paying for. They'll reimburse you for gas and meals. I promise."

"What sub do you want?" Steve said.

"Surprise me. They're all delicious. Give them the works, too," Jackson said and joined Cull, who was staring out the window.

"You alright? You've been quiet." Jackson leaned back and sighed. "This is going to be huge for us."

"For you. I'm not sure where I fit in," Cull said.

"Your pictures will accompany the stories. We'll rerun a few choice ones on the app to build it up. We'll need your backlog of shots you never used." Jackson smiled at Cull. "We're in this together."

"Partners?"

Jackson sighed and stopped smiling. "We'll figure it out."

Cull went back to looking out the window as a Peterbilt crawled past to the gas pumps. He wondered where the driver was headed and what he was carrying. He wondered if he missed home and a good life he had to leave behind or if his life was shit and the road was a welcome companion.

Steve dropped subs on the table, handing Cull and Jackson a cup of soda each. "I have the receipt. Someone is paying me back for this."

"I'm not even hungry," Cull said.

Steve groaned. "Then why did you let me waste my money?"

Cull unwrapped his sub from the wrapper. "I'll eat it. Relax. Just making a fucking statement, kid."

Now he wanted to toss the damn sub on the floor and stomp on it while this young punk watched in horror.

"Let's talk about our split," Steve said.

"There's nothing to split. We haven't even had a meeting. I think we're getting ahead of ourselves," Cull said. He took a bite and frowned. "Does this have onions on it?"

Steve squinted. "You didn't say no onions. You said, the works."

"I'll pick them out." Cull sighed. Getting a free sub and then finding out there were onions on it was bad, just like this app deal. It was a tease. On the outside it looked like a great sub. Lots of meat. Delicious bread. Except...they'd put damn onions on it.

This app idea was a delicious sub. Cull being involved was going to be adding unwanted onions. He could feel it. He needed something stronger than a Coke to wash down his food.

"What type of stuff are we looking for?" Steve asked.

"The usual: Bigfoot sightings, UFO abductions, alligators in the sewers. Anything either fake or unverified," Jackson said between bites. "That will initially fill us up with content. The real kicker will be when people start using it for the intended purpose."

"What's that?"

"Squealing on their neighbors. Pointing out the bad businesses in their area. You see a drug deal going on? Call the cops…but post on our app first, so everyone knows. It will revolutionize the Internet and social media," Jackson said.

"It sounds shady, even for *The Hidden Truth* and us," Cull said.

Jackson waved his hand. "We'll let the lawyers figure out what's legal and in a grey area. For now, I have the idea and I need to know you can put the app together, Steve."

"Of course, I can. It'll take me a couple of days to get a working model running. There are a bunch of other bells and whistles we can talk about the rest of the ride, too. I see a few other great applications, especially when it comes to advertising. We'll be rich." Steve put down his sub. "I want half."

"Half of my sub?" Jackson asked.

Cull snorted. "The fucker wants half of the money. Even though there is no money."

"We'll split it four ways. Each of us and *The Hidden Truth*," Jackson said.

"Why not just do it ourselves?" Steve asked.

Jackson shook his head. "We have a built-in readership. A huge mailing list. A history for these types of stories. If we had to start all over, it would take us time and money we don't have. I just need you to put the theory down so I can get them to front the initial cash for this."

"They're never going to give you money for this. Marty is a prick. He'll take the idea and run it up the chain as if it's his own creation. You'll see. The guy is worse than the two of us combined," Cull said. He was starting to get a really bad feeling about all of this.

Neighbor turning against neighbor? People spying to get their fifteen minutes of Internet fame.

"You're wrong." Jackson sighed. "I guess we'll have to sell this to *The Hidden Truth*. Make it worth their time and money. We do all the heavy lifting, but we use their contacts to make a lot of money."

"Then what's the split?" Steve asked. "I'm doing all the heavy lifting."

Jackson stared at Cull and smiled. "Would you be good with ten percent? Honestly, we'll just need your pictures. The bulk are already archived so you'd have minimal actual work to do."

"Ten seems steep for no work," Steve said.

"Shut up. Cull and I have been doing this shit for years. We need him onboard for this to work."

"Ten percent of nothing is a great deal," Cull said and snorted.

"Then, we'll both get twenty percent for doing all the work," Jackson said to Steve.

Steve was about to protest when Jackson held up his finger. "It's my idea. I have the contacts to get us a meeting. Without me you're back to driving your shitty car around town and hoping your ex-girlfriend and her new boyfriend don't need a ride to the club."

"Fine." Steve looked dejected and went back to his sub. "The first thing I'm doing is posting about the moon landing. People need to know."

"People need to know what?" Cull asked.

"I know how it was faked. My uncle's friend's father worked for NASA. He knows the real story. I can't wait to blow the roof off of it," Steve said and smiled.

Cull checked a second time for onions. *How many fucking times have we reported that story over the decades? Poor kid. The wakeup call from life is going dropkick him right in the balls one of these days.*

CHAPTER 5

NASA Predicts Ten Days of Total Darkness across the Earth

"Marty, Gentlemen, will you let me have the room so I can speak to these three privately for a moment." The Big Boss had spoken and most of the rest of the men she brought with her made for the door as quickly as they could gather their folders and devices.

The shuffle and clatter were quite dramatic. Steve rose from the chair next to Jackson until the reporter put his hand on the boy's forearm and settled him back into the seat. Katherine Hemingway's proclamation to leave carried great power.

Cull appeared immune. He seemed quite enthralled with rubbing an itch under his nose. He smelled better after the shower, but was quick to appear in need of another one in the unforgiving humidity and blanket heat of Florida. Cull's "T" zone and the divots under both nostrils had a way of looking oily within moments of breaking a sweat. Jackson thought Cull probably started sweating while he dried off from the shower most days. By lunch, he usually smelled a bit like Florida water tasted.

Cull went to working the inside of his nostril with the knuckle of his thumb. Jackson rolled his eyes. He tried to remind himself that the man had agreed to ten percent just to keep this fragile ploy from blowing up on the drive to the meeting. That was something. Not quite clearing the slate from gambling away the car, but it wasn't nothing.

Cull gave his nose a rest finally and cut a smile before dropping his eyes back to his lap.

Jackson followed the line of sight which had prompted Cull's brief amusement between pronounced indifference. Marty still sat on the edge of the desk behind the Big Boss. Jackson frowned. Katherine tilted her head to peer at Marty from an angle. Her suit jacket and matching skirt were pinstriped and pressed in tight lines which reminded Cull of 1930's gangsters. Her grey-blond hair pulled flat to the curve of her skull up to a rock-solid bun. Even her skull cap of hair had lines which rivaled the pattern of her suit for perfection.

Her face and body were starting to go. She still worked out and probably ate a lot of green stuff, Cull could tell, but sun damage, loosening of the skin, and darker veins in her calves told the story of her miles. Cull bet she was glamour hot not that long ago. He had worked for her magazine for years and saw her a few times in passing, but had no memory of exactly how hot she used to be. Probably really hot though. He'd bet Jackson's car and his camera on it.

She hadn't opted for plastic surgery or dying her hair either. That was the kind of "fuck you" attitude Cull could get behind. She gave the middle finger to time and to society. She was about to give it to fucking Marty, too. That was going to make getting tossed out on his ass after this meeting totally worth it to Cull. He felt bad that Jackson still believed putting their fate in this Fuck You Witch's "merciful spirit" was going to work. He looked down into his lap again and waited for this sad pantomime to be over for all of them.

"Martin? Can you close the door on the way out, sir?"

Cull felt a laugh boil up in his throat, but choked it into a couple coughs. He then pretended to scratch his nose again.

Marty glanced at Jackson and then looked away. He blinked several times and surprised himself with how close he was to tears. "I'm the editor here, Ms. Hemingway. Shouldn't I be in on this?"

"You've been in on it and now I'm doing my job as owner for the rest of it." She turned her palm up toward the ceiling and pointed over her shoulder at the open door to the conference room. "If you enjoy being my editor on this particular piece of my media empire, then go edit. Now, please. My time is precious and this place is eating my time along with my money. And now my patience, too? Martin?"

Marty stood and swallowed several times. He weaved between stacks of file boxes, the desk, and a table stacked with more papers. He felt Jackson's stare on his back. This new kid out of nowhere witnessed this dressing down, too. Cull, that old bum, probably enjoyed it the most. Marty closed the door and willed for her to fire them all. He nearly prayed for it. The damn kid didn't even work there, and he got to stay in the room.

Katherine's entourage looked up at Marty and then back down at their phones.

Katherine turned her attention back to the trio. The boy and the photographer found something interesting between their feet to occupy their attention. Good enough. She preferred for most of the pack to heel. It saved time. Jackson met her eyes and that was fine, too. She could smell desperation on him like the salt in the air down here which played hell with her hair, if she let it, which she never did.

She addressed the reporter with his eyes up. "Listen. This magazine has turned into a white whale for me. You understand what that means?"

"More trouble than it's worth," Cull said without looking up.

"Exactly. Even if it wasn't the lawsuits, the bleeding bottom line seems to have no bottom. The thing is an embarrassment to the other networks and outlets I own. This place is not popular with the boards, which can be overlooked if money is coming in, which it is not. Worse though, it isn't popular with readers anymore either. That's far less forgivable."

"This app will change that," Jackson said.

She held up a hand and shook her head. "Look. I understand everything you've said. I get how new media works better than you can imagine. I'll even have my teams look at the skeleton of a proposal you've managed to put together on your drive in. We're also going to consider the legal and PR side of things too which you have woefully overlooked in your overly optimistic attempt to salvage your jobs. I respect your will to fight which is the only reason we are still in this room, but I don't respect it enough to sink my profits from good money into the white whale of *The Hidden Truth* or an app by the same name. That's simply not how this is going to work."

"How could it work then?" Steve asked.

He was looking at her now and she fought the urge to smile. "What do you mean?"

"You have people looking at the idea or you will," Steve said. "So, you haven't dismissed it completely. If we make it work, you wouldn't want us to go after it on our own. So, what will it take for it to work for you? All your teams have to sign off? All the risks have to be out of the way? What exactly?"

"If I was averse to risk, this place would have been closed a decade ago," she said. "I'm not interested in throwing good money after bad. And that's really what you need from me, otherwise you would go do this on your own, correct? You need my money and my connection. You need my support and my legal protection. You need me. I'm not convinced yet that I need *The Hidden Truth*, either in its new or old forms."

"But you're still considering the option," Cull said. He did not bother to raise his eyes. "We're still here, so what is the proof in the pudding you need? What is the bottom-line product you want to see to make it worth your time?"

"This nonsense about your cuts on the ownership for starters," she said. "We're not starting a new business. We're remodeling this one which I already own. The boards have particular cuts of the profits already contracted out. We're not cutting them out and even if I wanted to, I couldn't get your numbers past them. They'd rather bury this place under a mile of cement like radioactive waste."

"What would our cut be?" Jackson said.

"No cut," she said.

Steve began to stand, but Jackson grabbed his arm again.

"Wait," Jackson said to her and to him. As Steve sat, Jackson said, "We have to get something out of this."

"If you create a working prototype of the app, we can consider it," she said. "Right now, you got nothing and you want me to invest in that. If we take it on, you can have your jobs back."

"I don't actually work here," Steve said. "I'm not doing this for no cut."

"Then, don't do it," she said. "If we decide to take on the app after we have something to look at, I'll put all three of you on salary...back on salary. If it works close to what you claim it does and we can streamline the staff here as a result, I'll bring you back on with raises."

"We have to make the app without having jobs while we do it?" Jackson said.

"You were laid off yesterday."

Cull said, "We need to be reimbursed for our last trip, expenses, and travel."

She smiled and shrugged. "Sure. I'll even give you both two months' severance and that can be your seed money for your proto app. Make it count because *The Hidden Truth* is out of second chances now."

"You said 'both' as in both of them," Steve said. "What about me?"

"You don't work here and never have. Remember?"

Steve did stand and Jackson didn't bother to grab him this time.

Cull stood, too. "Listen, Katherine...ugh, Ms. Hemingway. Give one month of my pay to the kid as a retainer. You already have skin in this game. Give them a fighting chance at least. I'm going to get out of the way here, so they can tell you what resources they need to make this work. Give them that much at least."

She traced Cull up and down with her eyes. "Is that all then or is there more I can do for you before you step out, sir?"

"Yeah, look at some performance bonuses. If the thing works like Jackson imagines it will, then give some bonuses. Your board can still make money if it takes off even with some bonuses. Merit pay is a business kind of thing to do, right? If they produce, they get paid and I'll get paid for taking pictures like I've always done for this place."

Jackson swallowed and whispered, "Cull?"

"Resources and performance bonuses. Got it," she said. "Anything else?"

"Fire Marty," Cull said.

She let out a single laugh. "Really?"

"Sure." Cull walked past her toward the door. A few pages floated off the table behind him as he went. "If the app is the moneymaker, then streamline Marty on out. Make Jackson the editor for the new media version of *The Hidden Truth*."

"Close the door on your way out, sir."

Cull did. The men pressed against the walls of the hallway as Cull passed. Marty stood in his doorway and smiled at Cull. Cull nodded and smiled back. This seemed to make Marty's smile waver and the lines in his face deepened.

Cull made for the front door and the heat outside. He thought about the sandwich place up the street and wondered when the severance money would clear. He tried to formulate a plan for where he would go after Jackson gave up on the app. Probably before. Why wait around to watch him suffer and fail again? Cull couldn't quite think past a sandwich this afternoon and a drink or five or nine this evening in one of the beachfront bars.

CHAPTER 6

Animals at the Zoo Are Plotting a Coup, New Report Suggests

The apartment building was too noisy. Jackson snoring on the couch was distracting. The TV was on just loud enough to bother Steve, who was just trying to work.

As soon as he stood, the kitchen chair scraping across the worn linoleum, Jackson sat up and burped. "How's it going?"

"I need some air," Steve said and walked to the front door. He reached for his keys, but stopped. He was nearly out of gas and he didn't think a drive would do anything more than annoy him.

"Can you grab lunch while you're out? There's a deli right around the corner. They make really good burgers. I'll have the number three with no ketchup. Thanks," Jackson said.

Steve shook his head. Jackson frowned.

"I'm broke. I don't have gas in my car. My wallet is empty. You're still collecting a paycheck," Steve said. "I'm really close to having this app done, but I need...I need a fucking break, okay? All you do is watch MTV reality television and sleep. Wake up, dude. You're way too old to be watching *Teen Mom* and *Catfish* episodes. You could be helping me."

Jackson put his head down. "I get it. I do. You left home. You're starting to doubt what you're doing in Florida. You're crashing on the couch of a weird old guy who watches TV like a sixteen-year-old girl."

Steve laughed. "It's just...getting frustrating. I'm working for free and your damn boss doesn't seem like, even if I somehow get this app to do what you want it to do, she'll pay me for my time. This could get you and Cull a lot of money. *The Hidden Truth* could get rich off of this. I'll still be broke."

"You'll be taken care of. I promise."

"Cull said the same thing. Remember? He was going to share his severance. I haven't gotten a dime from him. In fact, I know for a fact you haven't spoken to him in days. What rock is he hiding under?" Steve was getting upset again. He kept eyeing the door, knowing the smart move was to leave and never look back. Maybe he could get a few passengers along the way and make enough for gas money.

"I'll give you money for food. I wasn't expecting you to pay for it," Jackson said and fished a twenty out of his wallet, shaking his head. "I need you to trust me. This is going to work."

"Anytime someone has told me to trust them it's usually followed by an ass-fucking. Trust me is what my girlfriend might've said the last time we talked…right before she fucked another guy."

Jackson smiled. "I'm not like other guys."

Steve shook his head. "Not at all. Guys your age watch CNN and the local news and bitch about the good old days. You're like a retarded teenager."

"You're not supposed to say retarded anymore. It ain't woke, son."

"We're in private. Stop trying to change the subject. I'm trying to think of a reason, any reason, I shouldn't take this twenty and get gas and see how close to Biloxi I can get," Steve said.

"Not very. That's a good reason not to, and I feel like we're close," Jackson said and put up his hands when he saw the look on Steve's face. "*You're* close. I get it. You're doing the heavy lifting, as you like to say. At this point, I've sold it as best as I can, but the bottom line is you getting the damn thing to work."

"I'm really close. I just need to figure out a thing or two. I can't do it now, though. I need a break." Steve held up the twenty. "I'm going to get some food and take a walk to the beach. Clear my head. Figure this shit out before I lose my mind." He looked around at the empty takeout containers and Jackson's clothes strewn around the small living room. "Can you please clean this place up, too? You also live like a sixteen-year-old girl."

Jackson laughed and dropped back down on the couch. "Bring me back a burger. Take your time. There's always tomorrow to work on this, right? We have until Monday to get them something. Anything."

It was Friday.

Steve left, going down the rickety wooden steps of the apartment and heading north, not knowing where the deli Jackson talked about was located. He lived above a great place, Kokomo's Cafe, but it was closed this late in the day. Steve was starting to gain weight thanks to sitting outside drinking coffee and eating a meat-piled sandwich called a Cowabunga. Every day.

It could be worse. I'm not paying rent or for food, Steve thought, trying to stay positive.

He couldn't think of anything else that was positive. He was far from home and alone for the first time in his life. Living with Jackson wasn't a picnic. He was twice Steve's age, but there was a further gulf between them. Jackson had led an unpleasant life from what Steve could surmise. The guy had seen some really bad shit. It wasn't that he talked about it, either. Steve could just tell.

Steve didn't want to end up like Jackson and Cull. Old guys in dead-end jobs trying to scrape a few bucks together on a Friday night for cheap beer so they could sleep it off until their Monday morning commute.

He picked up a sandwich and a Coke at the deli four blocks up A1A, purposely not getting Jackson's food yet. He'd go back when he was done eating. It would give him more time outside and less in the stuffy apartment.

The sound of the waves crashing on the beach was inviting, so Steve strolled across the street to a crossover and down to the water's edge.

This close to the middle of Flagler Beach there was a lot of traffic both on the road and the sand. Families talking and laughing. Kids running in and out of the water. Older couples wearing shorts and absurdly large hats walking hand in hand. Two surfers trying to find a wave that didn't exist.

A group of teenagers began setting up a tent, volleyball net, and way too many towels a few feet from Steve, despite there being plenty of beach in either direction.

They don't even notice me. To them I'm the old guy with the goofy hat wandering the beach, he thought. He shoved the rest of his sandwich in his mouth and washed it down with the soda.

He'd need to go back and get Jackson's food and get back to work, trying to solve the problems in the app. It was working on his phone and he'd managed to sync the app to Jackson's and post a few fake story posts he'd copied and pasted from *The Hidden Truth* website.

It looked awful. Boring. On your phone the pictures were too small. There was too much information in these articles. Thousands of words no one would read on their phone or tablet. If they wanted this to work, they'd need to keep it simple and on the website, so people with laptops and desktop computers could log-in and add content.

It didn't look promising. Steve was way ahead of where he needed to be right now, but he wasn't telling Jackson or the Boss Bitch. Why should he? If everyone thought it was so easy for Steve to do, they might not see his value. They'd think any monkey could build this app.

He was also worried, once it was completed and went live, either nothing would happen with it or he'd receive no money for his hard work. Steve needed to pretend it was harder than it looked and build a couple of safeguards into the system, so he could shut it down completely or make it dormant. He needed some leverage in this gamble.

"Becky is such a whore, right? She's been sleeping with half of Flagler Beach. Wait until her husband finds out. You know she tried to pull Tommy into the bathroom at The Golden Lion the other night? I wish I could screw her over," one of the teenagers near Steve said.

He smiled. Oh, to have the problems of teens again instead of real grownup shit.

"She slept with Woody, the bartender, too. He denies it, but I see the way they look at each other," one of the other girls said. "I'd love to expose her. She thinks she's so damn cool because she's older. Maybe don't get married at eighteen a week after graduating. Maybe live a little first."

"She's living now, and she has a husband who works his ass off for her."

Steve stood. No one gave him even a glance. He was invisible to these kids. He hadn't realized before now, but in his twenties, he was considered old. Too young to hang with the Jackson crowd, too old for these kids.

All they had were big dreams, a full life ahead of them, and petty gossip that meant nothing in the grand scheme of things. Becky, whoever she was, would keep sleeping around and giving this group something to talk about every time they got together.

"Send her husband an anonymous message on Facebook or text him. That would screw her over."

"Too risky. Too much work, too. I'm not creating a new profile and all that just to catfish Becky."

"More like Whorebecky."

Everyone laughed. Steve made it to the wooden stairs. He'd need to get Jackson's food and head back. Try to figure out if there were any glitches in the app. Test it between his phone and Jackson's and make up a few shorter articles.

"Karma is going to bite her in the ass. Just watch. The truth always comes out."

Steve stopped and turned slowly.

The Hidden Truth always comes out....

Steve took out his phone and smiled. He walked over to the group, who still hadn't noticed him. "Hey, guys, you got a second?"

They all stared at Steve.

He held up his phone. "I overheard you talking about someone named Becky. She seems like a real slut. Am I right?"

It got a few chuckles from the crowd.

"Anyone want to test a new app for me? It's free right now. We're trying to get content for it. You'd all be a big help," Steve said.

"What do you need from us?"

Steve grinned. "I need you to download the app to your phones and start telling the world what a piece of shit Whorebecky is."

CHAPTER 7

Flagler Beach Strangler's Secret Vault of Trophies Discovered During Storage Unit Auction

Marty walked out of his house for the fourth time. He stopped again in the driveway next to his Lexus and patted his pockets.

"You've got to be kidding me." Cull tried to wipe sweat from above his eyes, but ended up rubbing the salty burn in deeper.

He had had the air conditioner and engine off ever since pulling up to the curb. The '78 Chevelle was on its last legs. Cull didn't even know they made a '78. Judging from how it ran, they probably shouldn't have.

Through palm fronds spilling over a muddy concrete wall, Cull saw Marty finally give up on whatever he may have forgotten this time and actually get in his car. He was almost surprised Marty was actually going this time.

The Lexus backed out of the drive and the rear wheels curved away from Cull's spot. Damn it. He thought he had the right end of the street. He slid down in the seat and peeked over the steering wheel. Marty cut the wheel madly to the right and ran up on the opposing curb, trying to get pointed in the right direction.

"Dumb ass." Cull scratched under his nose with one knuckle. "Same way you steered the paper into a brick wall."

Marty bounced off the curb and drove to the stop sign where he made a left.

Cull pulled on black, rubber gloves which clung tight to his skin. The sweat made them stubborn to pull into place and he had to wiggle his fingers out to the tips. He lifted his camera off the split leather of the passenger's seat.

The door ground on its hinges before it hammered closed. Cull glanced up and down the block, but saw no one. He ducked under the fronds and dodged between the concrete block wall and the power pole.

Someone had carved a swastika into the tarred wood of the pole. They had the bars going in the wrong directions toward one another. Below the retarded Nazi's bungled carving, someone had carved: *I hope ur muther's asshole falls off.*

Cull reached the point where the concrete block gave way to white painted brick with a patchwork of openings to see Marty's pool and patio furniture. The pool water was low and slimy green. Some black mold grew up the walls above the low waterline.

Cull looked around again and eyed the windows for anyone spying on him. He saw no other movement and no eyes.

Marty's front and side yards looked mowed, but the back yard behind the brick appeared overdue.

Cull set his camera on top of the wall and used the decorative peep holes to climb up and swing his leg over. He gave a grunt and took a few deep breaths as he straddled the wall. After steadying the camera, he climbed over and hoisted the camera down.

Two frogs kicked against the exposed step trying to launch themselves up to the slimy surface. Cull raised the camera and took a shot.

He set the camera down on the pink tile walk as he pulled on the locked doors to the sunroom. Inside, spiders and roaches piled dead along the floor between bottles of chlorine, bags of cement, and a stack of cardboard file boxes marked "donate" in black marker script.

Cull knelt on the tile and took out his wallet. He opened on a few singles and thumbed through the cards. The credit cards were maxed and useless, but he still didn't want to destroy them. The license would work, but if he cracked the plastic across the picture, he couldn't buy beer on the road anymore in some states. He learned that the hard way. Library card from

Alabama could be sacrificed, but it was too flimsy. Why did he still have that? When had he even gotten it?

Marty might be pulling back in the driveway now because he realized he forgot his phone or his sunglasses or his adult diaper. Who knows?

Cull drew out an expired insurance card and went to work between the door and frame. The latch bent the card, but popped free. He collected his wallet and camera and slipped inside. Crunching on spider and roach husks, he opened a set of French doors and stepped into the air conditioning. He almost shivered as it struck his sweaty body and face.

He opened the drawers to the cabinet under the mounted flat screen TV. Game disks and Blu Rays. Every action flick for the last who knows how long? The next drawer was DVD box-sets of TV shows. *The Wire, Friends,* and every season of *How I Met Your Mother, Entourage, Game of Thrones. The Real World vs Road Rules*? Who the hell would want to watch that once, much less revisit it?

The last drawer was more DVDs and Blu Rays mixed together. *Eyes Wide Shut* and *Another 9 ½ Weeks* graced the top of the clutter. Underneath was the really dirty stuff. *Busty Angels from Behind volume 2* and *Too Young to Know Better: The Cheerleader Edition* topped the stack of secret titles.

Cull spread them out and snapped pictures. He stepped back and got the open drawer in the shot with a framed photo of Marty with his mother or grandmother in a wheelchair. He crouched and smiled in the frame, but the old woman in the chair looked like she had forgotten what a camera was.

Cull held up a copy of *BBW MILFs in All Positions.* The heavy woman on the cover was all folds in a side-ass shot. A muscled black dude railed her from behind over a kitchen counter in what had to be a trailer. Her mouth and eyes opened wide as she stared at Cull from the cover frozen in mid-pounding.

He considered it, but dropped it back into the drawer. Cull closed it with the toe of his shoe without bothering to put everything back.

He strolled through the kitchen. The pantry was filled with

cooking wines and cans. There were seven partially used bags of brown sugar and twelve boxes of Jiffy Cornbread Mix. The fridge had leftover Chinese and condiments. Cull walked up a curved staircase with his footfalls echoing off the walls. The guestroom/office had boxes piled along one wall and an open, empty filing cabinet next to an empty desk and bare mattress and box spring on the other.

Cull opened one of the brown cardboard boxes on the end and found it full of baby clothes including a pile of tiny socks. "I don't even know what that's about."

He walked through the master bedroom with an unmade bed and dirty clothes on the floor. Cull snapped a picture of a pair of tighty-whities with an impressive skid mark. He opened the medicine cabinet. Antibiotics. Pain killers of varying doses. Not enough to confirm an addiction. Cull took the pictures anyway and closed the cabinet.

Back in the bedroom, the third drawer in the dresser had women's underwear and a .45 handgun. Two, small cardboard boxes under the lacey bras contained blanks in one and hollow points in the other. Cull opened up the gun to see which ones Marty had at the ready. It was empty and in need of cleaning.

Cull took the pictures with the panties, gun, and ammunition spread across the dresser in an arrangement he knew would make the best shot. As he dropped everything back into the drawer, he gave a pair of red, silky see-throughs a sniff. Tangy. Used and not washed probably.

It was only after the drawer was closed again that it occurred to him Marty might be the one wearing them.

Cull rifled through the side table and the under-the-bed boxes. Lots of vinyl from eighties pop and nineties alternative. Dog-eared western paperbacks. A few Cull remembered and enjoyed. He hated to think that he and Marty might share any sort of interests.

He really wanted to find a dildo, but no luck.

One of the westerns was bookmarked. He opened to see where Marty left off and found a picture of a pig wearing black panties. It wasn't a developed photo, but something cut out of a book or magazine. He set it up next to a framed picture on the side table of Marty with some woman – too young to be his mother. Cull took the shot. He went through the other books finding panty clad sheep and women pleasuring various farm animals. Cull took pictures of all the bookmarks and then restored the under-the-bed box.

"Gold," he said.

He found a green lockbox hidden in the back of the closet under piles of discarded sport coats. It had a weak lock. Should have been easy to pick.

Cull took the box and slammed it into the bathroom floor three times. A crack traced across two of the aqua tiles. The lock cylinder drove into the box from the dented front. Cull flipped it open.

Almost a thousand dollars in tens and twenties. Cull folded the stack over and stuffed it into his back pocket. Rare baseball cards in hard plastic cases including a signed Carlton Fisk from 1975. He had two Pete Rose rookies, too.

Cull counted out forty-five silver coins in individual plastic sleeves. He could make more pawning these than he already had in cash and could probably pull it off in shops up the east coast where he wouldn't get caught. Probably. This would be the shit to tie him to Marty's house, though, and this theft.

If he took them and tossed them all in the trash, Marty would have the cops looking for this stuff and would never look for any other leads in the meantime. It would really fuck with his head, too.

Cull closed the box with cards and coins still inside and stuffed it back under the coats for Marty to discover later. Leaving them behind would fuck with his head as well.

Cull made his way through the house and into the sunroom. He stopped and opened one of the "donate" boxes. More baby clothes. Pink jumpers and dresses. *Used to be married? Maybe. Who hadn't been, right? Lost a baby? Who knows?*

Cull left without locking the door.

He scampered over the wall and fought the forty-year-old engine of the Chevelle into life. He whipped a U-turn in the street, leaving rubber, but not hitting curbs like Marty's Lexus. He headed south parallel to the coast away from St. Augustine and Elkton where Marty hid his porn, panties, and baseball cards.

He could taste metal and aspirin in the back of his throat as he turned toward the western outskirts of Palm Coast off the Five and the Palm Coast Parkway. He passed the shitty city golf course and the gated neighborhood next to a patch of swamp. Then, turned into Heather's neighborhood across from the church that still looked like the resort the millionaire pastor had bought it from. Reflected sunlight from the church sign danced over the upholstery.

He pulled up onto the curb and killed the engine. As black smoke coughed out the back and the car gave a few thumps before finally lying still, Heather stepped out onto the path with a robe wrapped around her. She had two bobby pins holding her bottle blond hair away from her face.

Cull checked his watch. Too early for the kids to be home and too late for her to still be in a robe.

Shit. He still had on the black gloves. He tore them off with a sound like a cartoon smooch. He tossed them under the seat and threw his weight into the door.

Cull stepped out to the creak of the hinges.

"What you want, Cull?"

"To keep money in my pocket instead of giving it to you."

"Wages are garnished. It never hits your pocket."

"Yeah, you're the mistake that keeps on taking."

"Should have thought about that before you stuck it in." Heather waved a hand over her robed body. "I mean your little pecker and the drugs you took, either one. Both cost you and me and your kids, you know."

"My first wife was smart enough not to get knocked up."

"I envy her every day."

Cull took Marty's cash out of his pocket and counted out most of it. He held it out in a wad and she took it. Cull lifted the camera with the other hand and took a picture.

"What gives, pervert?"

"I need a receipt if you decide to lie and say I didn't pay you."

As he put the camera back in the car, she thumbed through the money. "Are you selling again?"

"Pictures? Sure. I was never selling drugs."

"Really?"

Cull repocketed what little remained. "Yes, really. I never cared about you enough to lie to you."

She folded her arms over her chest with Marty's cash clutched in her fist. "New car? And I use that description loosely."

"I got some severance from the paper and needed to replace a car for a friend. This was the best I could do."

"So, canned again?"

"I've worked for the same place for twenty years now. Better than you and better than your damn boyfriend down at the Golden Lion, too, I believe."

She rolled her eyes and pushed her tongue against the inside of her lower lip in the way that made Cull's fists clench and his balls draw up against his body. She said, "Well, I guess I should expect child support in cash or not at all some months for a while."

"Woody could chip in some since he's been sticking it in."

"He sticks it in good, too, Cull. You should get some pointers from him."

"I just wish you'd fuck around outside of Flagler Beach. You got all of Florida, you know. I hate having one less place to drink based on who you're seeing this week."

"Longer than a week and longer than you."

"We were together longer than you and Woodrow."

"When I say 'longer,' I don't mean how long we were together." She eyed his crotch and shook her head.

Cull grabbed his crotch and shook it until she stopped looking.

Heather turned her eyes up to the sky. "Are you going to sell more of that serial killer shit you were collecting?"

"I already sold most of it and lost the storage unit in an auction. All that great stuff is gone now."

"Creepy."

"It wasn't all serial killers. True crime and murderabilia is a great market. Kept us afloat through your shopping when we were together."

"Doesn't get less creepy the more you defend it."

Cull turned away. "Be sure to spend a little of that on the kids."

"You want to see them some time?"

"After all you've told them about me? Wouldn't want to scare them or disappoint you by showing up. Tell Woody's giant dick I said hello and I'm sorry...sorry he couldn't find anyone better."

Cull closed the car door and watched her walk back up her path. She closed the front door without affording him a glance back.

Cull sighed as he stared at the face of the mega church in the rearview.

He took the memory card out of his camera and replaced it with a fresh one. He slid the one with pictures from Marty's house down into his sock. "Damn. I'll need to get the money pic off of there. And explain where I got cash. Money shot...ha!"

As he started the car, his phone chimed. It was a Google Alert about Hidden Truth. Jackson had showed him how to set them and now Cull didn't know how to turn the shit back off.

He usually scanned for his name and then deleted the messages. Most of the time it was "end of the world" predictions from a Pastor Cull up in Tennessee. Such a thing was right in the wheelhouse of their usual investigations, but this dumbass made fire and brimstone boring.

The e-mail opened on a free trial offer for the Hidden Truth app.

"Holy shit." Cull glanced up into light reflecting off the massive metallic cross in his mirror. "They actually did it?"

He tried to close the message, but ended up following the link instead.

"Shit."

He closed three ads and then tried to close the site. It started to download.

"Motherfucker."

The app popped open on a featured story about a father killing his kids at the youngest's first birthday. He recognized his pictures from a back issue of the magazine.

A "Get Latest Reports Now!" pop-up jumped into view just as Cull tried to click on the story.

"Son of a Bitch."

He paused over headlines of affairs and drug habits and theft and fetishes.

"How many people are using this?"

He clicked one of the headlines tagged with "Flagler Beach" Cull threw his head back and laughed. Woody and some other dude supposedly tag-teamed a young newlywed named Becky. *So rich.*

He set his phone aside and drummed the steering wheel. He wanted to tell her, but she would turn it around on him. It would hurt more when she found out on her own later. If she found out Cull knew before her and didn't say anything, that would fuck with her more.

Cull laughed again and grabbed his crotch as he pulled away from Heather's house.

CHAPTER 8

15 Ways to Get All the "Strange" You Ever Wanted and Never Get Caught! – #9 Will Blow Your Mind!

She woke up to the sound of the Senator scrambling out of bed. He was trying to keep his voice down, but he growled into his phone like someone was strangling him. His bare ass was clenched tight enough to shit fresh diamonds. He was old, but had a runner's body. He did charity half marathons in his district when he was trying to appear to be a caring man before the people. That's where Anna met him – as a volunteer, not as a fellow runner.

Anna cast the blanket off to let him see the goods. He might cut his phone call off and give one more go before they parted for the morning and another couple of weeks. Their meet-ups were top secret, but he was fun for a night or two.

He slammed a fist into a wall and growled. "Well, find out who it is, so we can deal with it, goddamn it!"

She realized he wasn't being quiet to keep from waking her. He was ready to murder someone, and he didn't want her to hear the details. He was wishing she wasn't in the room anymore. She rolled out of bed and stuffed her green dress into her "bail out" bag. She pulled out a pair of sweatpants and a heavy shirt without bothering to locate underwear.

"No, not yet," he said. She could tell by the change in his voice that he had turned to look and see where she was. "We'll try to smother it before it comes to that. Find out who has to be dealt with and then make the deal. I want nothing coming back to me. My fingerprints are nowhere on it. Right. I'll call you next when I can."

He hung up.

Anna thought, *Shit. It's me. Someone found out about me. Life is going to get complicated.*

"I got stuff to deal with. Work stuff. You'll see yourself out as soon as you get ready?"

"Of course."

"Don't try to contact me."

"Understood."

He grabbed up his own clothes and walked out of the room without collecting his bag, toiletries, or anything. Even the laptop stayed open on the desk in the corner. She heard him dressing in the hallway and heard the front door open and close shortly after.

Whatever it was, it was bad. He didn't even spend his usual forty-five minutes primping and perfecting. That didn't include the half hour shower to wash her off of him before he left. He skipped that, too. Not good. She was never going to hear from him again.

She hauled her bag up onto the unmade bed and set her clothes out. She took the time to lay out cotton bra and panties. The fancy thong and lacey bra were for the night before. Probably their last night.

She pulled her blond hair back from her face and behind her ears. If the thing with the senator was over, it might be time for a real change. She needed a new game and new distractions. Time to put on a new hustle. Anna decided it was probably time to go red again.

Anna walked naked to the desk and sat on the soft cushion of the chair. It wasn't his real work computer. He wouldn't bring that and leave it at a rental. It did have the same password though. If he didn't want his secrets getting out, he probably needed to be better about that.

She fired it up and typed in his first dog's name and "69" after it. She wasn't sure what that password said about him, but she was just the recently fired part-time mistress, so what did it matter to her now?

None of the files on the desktop were new. She had looked through all the juicy stuff there was to see during previous visits. Plenty to get him in embarrassing PR situations, but nothing illegal really. All of that was probably on the work computer, with the same password.

She ran a search on him, but nothing came up. Maybe it was contained. She went ahead and perused the tabloid sites anyway.

Anna squinted. She went to her bag and took out her phone. It took a while for the app the download. That usually meant it was a big program. She'd probably have to delete it right after to save memory.

While she waited, Anna googled "Hidden Truth App." It hadn't been out long, but there was buzz. Sounded like another social media fad. Another "The New Facebook" which would implode in a week. It sounded nastier than 4Chan though, so this had to be good and dark for a morning of breaking up with a svelte senator.

She scrolled through a few more search results. "Holy shit. What is happening? 'Call out culture' on steroids. Hmm, sounds delicious."

She opened the app and explored. It took a while to unpack. She tried to calculate how long it would be before someone on the senator's private payroll came through to clean out the place with her included.

Stories popped onto the feed faster than she could read them. She thought she was reading confessions of rape, murder, incest, affairs, etc. Then, she saw people were reporting each other. More people were piling on, adding details to previously reported stories.

You could search by town, state, or region. You could search by name or crime category. You could even search by specific sexual act or fetish.

She looked up one of the senator's secret sins. She had become quite good at it with practice. Turned out it was more common than she thought. Anna wasn't sure she wanted to know that.

She looked up the Senator's name. There was a listing, but it was marked as "pending." Lots of people had already bookmarked it. This had to be it. Maybe they just wanted money and then it would go away. That could be what the phone call was about. They were going to contact the app makers and smother it before it got out. Or the Senator could have been upset about something else and didn't even know about this. She thought maybe she should call him or his people about it, but then realized that was a terrible idea.

"Hidden Truth? Couldn't be the same one…."

She returned to the computer. It was the same as the tabloid.

"What are you up to now, Aunt Carmella?"

This had to be squashed. Her "godmother" didn't exactly owe her anything nor did she want Anna around ever, but she had dragged Anna in by involving the Senator in whatever this "call out" app was that she put together.

Was it blackmail? That was *exactly* her family's style, but not through the legit businesses. At least Anna hadn't thought so. Even that murdering bitch wouldn't do something like that out in the open. And not to a sitting senator. She was evil, but she wasn't stupid.

Anna opened an e-mail and typed: *Dear Carmella….*

She stopped for a long moment and then decided to change the opening. No reason to provoke the crazy bitch while she needed something from her.

Anna added: *I've been thinking about my late mother and I….*

She stopped again. Still no good. Same problem. She deleted the whole line.

Anna typed: *I need to talk to you about the Hidden Truth App as it pertains to….*

She stopped again. She couldn't type the Senator's name in an e-mail. This was a no-win situation. She was going to have to go see the bitch in person. This was the worst idea of all, but her life was going to get very complicated if the "pending post" on the heavily bookmarked notice was about her.

Carmella didn't want to see Anna ever, but the bitch especially didn't want anything to do with dragging Anna into her life and business. Dropping the post might be worth making Anna go away.

"There's no other way," Anna told herself.

She tried to look up which state the bitch was in. Anna

realized it could be overseas and there would be no getting to her then.

Anna smiled. That wouldn't be so bad of a trip. She decided that she was definitely going back to red.

CHAPTER 9

Mafia Boss Bought the Loch Ness Monster

"You promised me money. Something. I need to eat. Gas is expensive in Florida. This is bullshit," Steve said.

Jackson didn't have time for this. He closed his eyes and rubbed his temples. Katherine and her new cronies would be entering the boardroom any minute. "We need a unified front, Steve. Show her we're on the same page. We won't take less money."

"Did she offer us money?" Steve asked, slapping the table with both palms.

"Not in so many words. Nothing definite like a number, but if this app keeps growing like I predict it will, she'll be swimming in dough." Jackson wanted her to enter the room, so he could get on with it and stop Steve's incessant talking for even a few minutes. Night and day all he'd been talking about was his big payday and when it was going to arrive.

"I knew I shouldn't have listened to you when you handed all of *my* hard work over without settling on a number. I really got screwed, like that other guy from Facebook. Anyone remember his name? Nope. Wasn't there a partner in Microsoft or Apple, too? All of the real workers, the actual brains, were bumped out while the figurehead stayed on to reap the rewards. It isn't fair." Steve was up and pacing next to the table now.

He stopped at the window and spotted Katherine down the hall. A group of men stood farther away, seeming to wait on her. It looked like Katherine was in a heated discussion with some other woman. The glass and distance obscured his view, but the woman had red hair and wildly blue pants. Almost neon. The poor redhead was probably having her ass handed to her the same way Steve was about to.

"You're ranting for nothing. Believe me, she'll do the right thing. We're going to get paid. It might not be a big chunk of money at first, but it will be enough for you to get your own place. Upgrade your wheels. Buy actual food instead of fast food each meal. Just shut up for a few minutes so I can think," Jackson said.

Steve stepped away from the window. "I swear, if she screws me over today, I'm going to pull the plug on this."

Jackson opened his eyes and frowned. "What are you talking about?"

Steve smiled. "I put in a special passcode. Only I know it. I can remotely kill it. Shut the bitch down. It will wipe out all of my work, but be worth it if she doesn't pay me."

"You can't do that. We need to negotiate with her, not threaten. We've come too far. The app works. It really works." Jackson was up and pacing the other side of the table now, mirroring Steve.

"I can do whatever I want. I created it."

Jackson stopped walking and pointed at Steve. "Wrong. I created it. You made it a reality. We're in this together."

"I did the heavy lifting."

"I know. You always say that. I get it. I really do. But...we can use the kill switch as leverage." Jackson grinned. "You're brilliant. We have her over a barrel. What's the password?"

"No way. I don't trust you."

"Seriously? I don't want to give this up so easily. With the password they have to give us money. Lots of money. They'll see they'll still get paid. Big money, too. Katherine is a smart woman. She knows this is a cash cow. But if there's a kill switch in the system, she won't play ball with us. She'll let you destroy it and find someone else to do the work, unless...." Jackson laughed. "It's so simple."

"What is?"

"Cull is the wild card she won't be expecting."

"What do you mean?" Steve sat back down. He looked tired to Jackson.

"Give me the passcode and I'll give it to Cull. That way

someone outside this room has it. For safekeeping. In case she does something she might be capable of."

Steve shook his head. "No way. I don't trust Cull. Where is he, anyway? He hasn't been around in days. He isn't even interested in any of this. He took his severance and left. He never gave me a dime, either, like he promised."

"Do you know how Katherine got the seed money for this venture back in the day?"

Steve shook his head again.

"Ever heard of The Family?"

"My grandmother used to watch *All In the Family* and *The Golden Girls*," Steve said.

"It's the New Jersey Mob. They gave Katherine's father the initial startup for the paper. They really control all of this. As long as they're getting their cut, they leave everyone alone. I'm sure by now they're counting on x number of dollars each month thanks to the app. If you shut it down, you'll make some people very unhappy," Jackson said.

"Holy shit. You got me involved with the Mob?"

"No. The Family. They're worse. We need to give Cull the passcode or we have nothing to bargain with," Jackson said.

"I can't...this doesn't feel right."

Jackson could hear muffled talking coming down the hallway. They didn't have much time. He pulled out his phone. "Tell me. Please."

"Don't screw me over." Steve stared at Jackson's phone. "I trust Cull less than I trust you at this point."

"Cull has my back. He also has your best interests in mind, too. Don't let his asshole exterior fool you. He's a loyal friend and he'll do the right thing when the time comes," Jackson said.

He could see shadows through the door. Katherine was here.

"Fine. The password is Monique69."

Why does everyone still use 69 in their passwords?

"Should've known you'd use your girlfriend's name," Jackson said.

"Ex-girlfriend. I'm going to rub her nose in all the money I get from this shit."

"I don't suppose I need to know why you put 69 at the end."

Steve grinned. "It was definitely a favorite of hers."

"I bet it still is." Jackson didn't watch for Steve's reaction to the dig. He sent Cull a message with the passcode, but not what it was for. Just to not erase it. "We're all set. I would let me talk. See if I can negotiate a deal, so they don't have to know anything about the kill switch."

"Starting the meeting without me? Everyone, sit," Katherine said. She went to the head of the table but stood. "Let's make this quick. I have another meeting in fifteen minutes."

Six people from management sat down at the table. Jackson noticed Marty wasn't one of them.

"What's this about?" Katherine asked Jackson.

"It's about me," Steve said.

Jackson shook his head. He wanted Steve to shut up and let him talk first.

Katherine looked more amused than angry. "I'm listening. Stan, was it?"

"Steve," he said through gritted teeth. Jackson knew this was going to go poorly.

Jackson cleared his throat. "Steve is the man who actually put the app together. The reason it's running, in fact."

"Then, why do we need you?" Katherine asked.

"I created it," Jackson said, trying to keep her gaze and failing. Instead he focused on a nick on the table.

"Then, I thank you. You work for me. The app is mine. I did all the proper paperwork and legalities needed for it to work. Right?" Katherine drummed her fingers on the back of her chair, which she was standing behind. "I'm not sure why I'm here."

"I did all the heavy lifting," Steve said.

Jackson stifled a groan. If he heard that stupid phrase one more time, he'd punch Steve in the face.

"I feel like we've had this conversation before," Katherine said. "If there's nothing new to add, I think we're done."

"What about getting paid?" Steve asked.

"You're not on my payroll. In fact, I have no idea why

you've been allowed in the building." Katherine turned to leave and her board members stood.

"I have a kill switch set up in the app," Steve said and smiled. "If I don't leave this room with everything I want, I'll simply engage it and your app will be gone. Is that what you want?"

Katherine laughed. "Of course not. But you're not getting another dime from me until I'm sure this is a long-term solution. I can't pay you a truckload of money on an app that will be MySpace in six months. You have to understand where I'm coming from."

"I need a contract. Something binding," Steve said.

"You're not getting anything from me." Katherine turned to the closest member of her board. "Go get security. I don't want this gentleman in my building anymore."

Steve held up his phone. "I swear, I'll take it down before you've had a chance to see its full potential. I won't just pause it, either. The kill switch deletes every file. It will all be gone. I'm not bluffing."

Katherine smiled. "What, exactly, would that prove? If you delete the app, we'll just build another one. We'll find a way and then you can bet your sweet ass you'll never see a dime from this. Put your phone down. Let's talk."

She pulled out her chair as if to sit and shot Jackson a dirty look.

I wish he'd let me speak first, Jackson thought. This was unraveling at an alarming rate. He knew Katherine was never going to negotiate in good faith with Steve now that he'd made this stupid play. *Time to fix this one way or another.*

"Maybe we should all take a break. Think about this," Jackson said.

Katherine smiled. "Take all the time you want. Have a seat. We'll order in lunch."

Jackson knew she was stalling, waiting for security. Steve had fucked up and now Jackson was going to lose his job and his app. If they had this meeting at the paper office in Flagler, there wouldn't have been hardly any staff, much less security.

"I'd rather stand," Steve said, trying to look defiant as he held his cell phone at arm's length.

"Are you planning on blowing up your phone and killing everyone in the room or just turning off an app? Your pose seems so dramatic," Katherine said.

Steve pulled his arm to his chest, but switched hands and stuck the phone back out. "I don't want anyone near it or I'll shut it down. I promise."

"What do you want?" Katherine asked.

"I want money."

"I'll put you on the payroll. How does ten bucks an hour sound?"

Steve shook his head. "I don't want a job. I want fifty thousand in cash."

"And you'll sign over all rights to the app?"

Steve nodded.

"Would you rather have a hundred grand? What about a million?" Katherine asked with a smile. "I'll give you a blank check and you fill it out. Tack on a bunch of zeros if you want. It doesn't really matter. You know why? Because you don't own any rights to the app. I do."

Security barged into the room.

Jackson took a step toward Steve.

"I warned you," Steve said and swiped the screen on his phone. "Now it's all going away."

"Not quite," Jackson said and yanked the phone from Steve's hand.

"What are you doing?"

"Saving my app. It's still my idea and you're not going to screw me out of this," Jackson said. "I know the password. I'll go in and change it. Steve's done enough for us. We don't need him anymore, but it would be nice if we gave him something before he left. It would be fair."

"Fair? How about this, Jackson? You fix the app and make sure this never happens again. My security delivers your former associate to the police waiting downstairs and he's tossed on the street and issued a restraining order for me and my building and my employees. In return, I don't send him to jail. I'm sure he can't make bail since he has no money. No future. Nothing," Katherine said.

"Jackson, don't do this," Steve said as two security guards grabbed his arms.

"Let's go to lunch, Jackson. I think it's time your loyalty was rewarded." Katherine smiled.

Jackson sent a message to Cull to ignore the message he'd sent and pocketed Steve's phone.

CHAPTER 10

Crooked Cops Cover for Illuminati Sex Ring – Warning: Graphic Images

Cull checked his phone as he trudged through the bushes and undergrowth. He needed to get the car to Jackson before it died on him, and he needed help getting these damn notifications shut off on his phone.

The app dinged every minute and sometimes more. Cull hated it, but he couldn't keep himself from looking. This stuff was too good, and it had spread away from Florida like a tidal wave. Some of it was in foreign languages, but there was a lot of juicy stuff in English still.

A couple in Arizona was torturing children, the wife's aunt said. A cop in Seattle was letting hookers off in exchange for blowjobs in his car. His ex dropped the dime on him. *Big deal. He should let them off. It's the only gentlemanly thing to do really.* Housewife in Salt Lake City was sleeping with leaders of the LDS church in exchange for drugs and money. A half dozen people told versions of that same story. None of them quite matched up.

Nice.

Cull pocketed his phone and lifted his camera. Finished houses on a clover of looping roads lined up to his left on the other side of a reedy drainage basin. To his right, barren, red dirt marked the cleared ground for a new development.

He angled toward the lake through the trees and the flashing lights to his right above the lake. Bugs nipped at his neck and sunlight through the trees burned at his scalp. He needed a hat. Maybe one of those cool PI hats.

He needed the damn rednecks to do their killing closer to

the resorts. Daytona was always a nice, close goldmine of sordid stories. Cull was in a patch of wilds a few miles inland from Daytona Beach though. He guessed he was west of Ormond and DeLand, too. Why were his contacts at the Daytona PD handling this one anyway?

He found the yellow tape and walked along as uniforms he didn't recognize eyeballed him.

"Stay behind it," one of them said.

"I got this one." Randy with his belly testing the buttons of his uniform held up a hand and moved between Cull and the others on the inside of the tape.

"Great spot for a murder or malaria. How'd you find this one?"

"Double murder actually and the dude that did it was kind enough to wait for us to show up."

"That was sweet of him." Cull waved his camera lens toward the water's edge and a sheet of rumpled plastic. "I made it in time to catch the stars of the show?"

"Forensics just finished. They're coming to load the bodies now. A few minutes out."

"Forensics can't take too long, if the killer hung out and waved you down. How much evidence do you need?"

"You'd be surprised."

Cull shook his head. "I've been around a while. Very little surprises me. So, walk me over before the good stuff is cleaned up."

Randy rubbed his fingers together down by his thigh. "Love to. Do you have a ticket? Regular price today. No matinees in this economy."

"Tell me you're not wearing a body cam."

"Of course, I am. Forgot to turn the damn thing on is the thing."

Cull reached in his back pocket and pulled out the rest of Marty's money. "I'm about twenty-five short. Between paydays at the paper. More than you'll have if you turn me away."

Randy snatched it from him and stuffed it his shirt pocket above his nametag. "Damn, Cull, you're as subtle as a cock on a coed."

He lifted the tape and Cull ducked under. "Looks like there was a matinee after all."

"Don't push your luck." Randy waved at the others as he walked Cull toward the water. "He's freelance with the department. We're good."

The others didn't look convinced.

Randy knelt and pulled back the plastic. The women were pale and their eyes bloody red from burst capillaries. Tee shirts over bikini tops.

"Pull the plastic off them. I'm here for the goods."

Randy sighed, but he obliged.

One body in cutoffs with the white pockets showing under the thready edges. The other wore skinny acid wash jeans that had zippers at the ankle. One still wore her open toed sandals and the other had on muddy sneaks.

The guy who killed them didn't have any fun with them first.

There hadn't been enough time for their necks to bruise yet. That might have to be Photoshopped in later then.

Cull clicked pictures. "You got names?"

"Don't get me in the shot." Randy pointed to cutoffs and then at skinny jeans. "Debbie Sanders, the wife of the killer, Edward Sanders. And her sister, Reece Puscas, Edward's side chick."

"No shit?" Cull knelt and took more shots with the lake in the background. He caught some cleavage on both. Wanted to adjust the tops to get more bang for the buck. Normally, Randy was one who could be pushed, but Cull had already short-changed him and asked for the plastic all the way off. Randy seemed a little edgy. Cull wanted to save his chits for something later. Daytona was a goldmine after all. There would always be something later. "Were they strangled?"

"According to Edward, the wife went ape shit on the sister and smashed her head on a rock here by the water while he was trying to pull them apart."

"You got the rock?"

"Already bagged and logged."

"Roll her head, so I can get the wound."

"Are you fucking with me?"

Time to cash those chits early. "Come on, Randy. Short time. Just do it quick."

Randy huffed and rolled Reece's head to the side. A small crater disrupted her dye job in the back. Cull had hoped for more. Leaves and dirt in the hair with the cop's hand holding the head added something though. Cull snapped off several shots.

"Keep me out of the shot and hurry up."

"Got it."

Reece's head still faced away after Randy let go.

"Let's go then, Cull."

He took a few more pictures including Randy in the shots. "How did the wife die, according to poor Eddie?"

"Says she came after him and he held her down by the throat. Says by the time he let go, she was choking and wouldn't stop. He tried CPR, he says, but couldn't get air in."

"You believe that shit?"

Randy shrugged as he stood with an effort. "Autopsy will tell, I guess. Thinks she was already dead by the time he called 911, he says."

"Takes a hell of a lot to strangle someone all the way to death. Not the kind of thing you accidentally do, from what I understand."

"Could have crushed the bones and she choked to death. Smarter body men will figure that out. We got the guy, so my part is done and so is yours. Let's go."

Cull looked around. "You still got him here?"

"Up in a car where the street for the new development ends. Next to where all their cars are parked."

"Walk me by on the way out." Cull lifted his camera.

"Fuck you. I'll throw you in the lake, if you want."

"Come on, man. This is what we do."

Randy chewed at the inside of his cheek and looked up the slope past another cluster of officers. Randy pulled the plastic back over the bodies. "Okay, but after you take a couple pictures, I'm going to rough you along and shove you out from under the tape to make it look good."

"Sounds like a plan."

Cull's phone chimed as they walked. He sighed, but had to look anyway. It was a text this time from Jackson.

Monique69?! Cull laughed out loud and Randy looked at him. Cull didn't bother to explain. Sounded more like a sex bot than anything Jackson might be into. Why not e-mail it to himself, if it was something that needed keeping? Even Cull knew how to do that.

Another notice popped up from Hidden Truth. More stories, of course, and then an announcement of premium memberships coming soon.

What a racket!

"How did the wife find out about the cheating? How'd they all end up out here supposedly?"

"One of those Ashley-Madison sites, I guess. The wife went on and everything the two of them had done was listed. Even the fact that they were meeting here today. That was according to the dude anyway. Would have to ask the wife and she ain't talking."

"Do you have her phone?"

"Bagged and tagged. If I hear someone say what site it was, I'll pop you a message. It was Hidden Meet-ups or Hidden Secrets or the Dirty Truth or something like that. People tell each other's secrets on it apparently. Like some revenge doxing site."

Cull looked down at the phone. "Was it the Hidden Truth?"

Randy shook his head. "No, that's the name of your rag, right? I'll find out and let you know."

Cull pocketed his phone as they passed the other officers and stepped into the sun. A scruffy, skinny dude with a wife beater, tattoos, and goatee sat cuffed in the back of one of the PD's Range Rovers. His bare feet hung out over the running board with two uniformed cops flanking him.

Other police cars, a pick-up truck, and a Prius sat along the dusty street spotted by foundations and gravel drives.

"Like out of central casting." Cull raised his camera.

"Make it look good," Randy said.

Cull snapped off several pictures. Edward turned his face away into the shadows of the vehicle.

Randy took Cull by the arm and hauled him toward the tape. "That's enough of that. Move your ass along before I arrest you, too."

Randy lifted the tape and shoved Cull under. He used a little more force than Cull expected and he struggled to keep his footing. Maybe Randy was pissed about being shorted twenty-five.

Randy spoke up behind him. "Sorry, guys. That guy's freelance with the department. Doesn't know his boundaries, I guess."

Cull took a few shots of the civilian vehicles before moving along. He walked along the barren roads of the development trying to circle back to his car. Jackson's car, he guessed really, if he ever got it to him.

The phone chimed again. Cull wiped sweat from his eyes and scratched at his nose. It was too hot for surfing other people's dirt, although he really ought to add the ending to this little love triangle in for the readers. He supposed that was what these pictures were for.

He needed to get back to Jackson and figure out what was going on.

He checked his phone. Another text from Jackson saying to never mind.

"Guess he figured out it was a sex bot." Cull scrolled through the newest stories on the app.

CHAPTER 11

Sunken Neanderthal City Found Off the Coast of Jacksonville Beach

Steve tapped the empty glass, but the bartender knew to ask for money first.

With a groan Steve tossed his last ten on the bar. Could this day get any worse?

He went to his pocket for the tenth time, but Jackson had kept his phone. Steve supposed he could call the police and tell them it had been stolen. Maybe get Jackson and his asshole boss in trouble, although by now everything important would be wiped out.

Jackson would know enough about the app to change or delete the kill switch buried inside. In his arrogance, Steve hadn't tried to hide it, either. He thought Jackson was fully on his side.

If you'd been smarter you would've held back all your rambling information about the app and what you were doing, he thought. Jackson knew all of it because he was always there. Watching Steve do the heavy lifting.

He'd been set up to work for free. No wonder he stayed with Jackson. The guy was slick. He'd come off like a fellow idea guy. A slacker trying to get the latest get rich quick scheme off the ground.

Jackson had successfully done it at the expense of Steve, who was in the wrong place at the wrong time.

The story of my life.

Without his phone he had no way to collect fares, either. No way to make any money. He was stuck in Jacksonville. It was an hour's drive to Flagler Beach to get his stuff, if Jackson would even let him to collect it. That dude had fucked him.

What about Cull? Where was he? That smelly bastard didn't seem like he was completely onboard with all of this. He hadn't bothered to show for the meeting today. The last time Steve had seen him he didn't seem too interested in the app or anything else. He just wanted his job back to take pictures and doctor photos.

Steve needed a game plan, for the first time in his life. He'd wasted the last few days. Weeks? It felt longer. He also had the nagging feeling, as much as he'd been screwed over, it didn't really matter. If he'd stayed in Biloxi, life would've gotten worse, too.

At least in Flagler Beach he'd had a purpose, even if only for a few days. It beat the alternative, which was still driving drunks around between casinos and getting chips for tips.

He stared at the new glass on the bar in front of him and the small pile of singles, all the money he had left. If he was lucky, he had enough gas to get a few exits on I-10 before he'd run out.

What was the worst-case scenario? Having to call his parents to drive over six hours one-way to pick him up or at least give him gas money to get home?

Biloxi was home and Steve hated the thought of it.

He'd thought he was on some grand adventure. He was going to get back at Her. Steve couldn't even bring himself to say or think of his now-ex's name. She was dead to him. She was gone.

If I beg, maybe she'll take pity and come get me, Steve briefly thought before shrugging it off and finishing his beer. Suicide was a better option than to beg that bitch to take pity on him. Even if she actually came, and did so without her new boyfriend, she'd never talk to Steve again. She hated how weak he was at times. What a slacker. No future.

Steve knew the app was the future and he was so pissed it had been taken away. One of his goals, besides money and fame, was to fly first-class into Biloxi and have a stretch limo cruise him around the old neighborhood so everyone could see how successful he was. Make sure his ex would know she fucked up and lost the best thing that had ever happened to her. Maybe he'd run into her at a restaurant with her new beau, and Steve imagined paying for everyone's dinner but hers. He'd hire strippers to hang out with him for the night. Get seen by the assholes he went to school with and show his parents he'd made something of his life, despite their negative attitudes. It beat dying in some nowhere town, full of closed restaurants, surrounded by drug addicts and meth cooks.

Deciding it was smarter to hold onto his last few singles instead of spending it on more beer, Steve left. He had no real place to go, but sitting at a bar in the middle of the day wasn't helping his mood.

Outside the bar, the sun tormented him, blinding his eyes and forcing Steve to run to his car and find his sunglasses.

He fumbled with his keys, realizing the only one he needed was the car key. The rest were parts of his past he'd never return to. Dreaming of limos and upset exes wasn't reality. The shitty impulsive move to follow two old assholes across the country was his reality.

Steve separated the car key from the rest and tossed them in the street.

Inside the car was about a million degrees, but he couldn't waste gas by using the air conditioning. He also couldn't cruise around the city and waste it, either.

Steve had nowhere to go thanks to Jackson.

Thanks to Katherine and *The Hidden Truth*.

Thanks to…*fuck it, thanks to everyone in my life. They've taken it all away. The last chance I had to make something of myself. They've proven to my shitty parents, former friends, teachers, that motherfucking Navy recruiter last year, and everyone I ever crossed paths with, what a fuckup I am.* Steve wished he had a gun. He'd like nothing better than to march into the offices of The Hidden Truth and shoot some people in the head. Go out in a killing spree, even if he took one or two himself in the shootout, going out himself.

Show the world what he was capable of.

Only…he wasn't capable of doing it. Was he? Even if he magically had a gun, he wasn't going to do anything past fantasize about shooting an office up.

No, he needed a better plan.

Steve wiped the sweat off his face a few minutes later.

He had nothing.

It wouldn't be worth the gas to drive back to Jackson's place and wait to kick his ass. Steve was also honest enough to know, despite being twice his age, Jackson looked like he'd been a fighter and tough guy back in the day. If he'd driven all the way to Flagler and wasted the rest of his gas only to get a black eye and lose what little pride he had left, he'd need a gun to put in his mouth.

Instead of losing more weight sitting in the hot car, Steve got back out. He had a fleeting moment of wanting to toss the key on top of the car, so someone would steal it, but he might still need it.

He started walking, hoping inspiration or a bus would hit him.

When he thought back to the car trip from Biloxi to Jacksonville, his brain hurt so he tried to block it all. He thought about good times, like his first groping of boobs and how much he loved chocolate chip mint ice cream on a hot day.

It didn't do any good. He wanted to scream at everyone he passed on the street. Tell them their lives didn't matter. Let them know it was all a lie. Did they think they were safe in their cubicles at work? They weren't. Not even close.

They were all wandering around oblivious to his troubles. What did they care anyway? A woman wearing a slick pantsuit with her hair and makeup perfect despite the heat wandered by, tapping manicured nails on her phone.

Steve wanted to grab her by the arm and yell in her face, even though she had nothing to do with his shitty life. Maybe she was part of the problem. Part of this system. Maybe she had terrible, hidden secrets that would destroy her.

He let her keep walking and took a long look at her ass as she went by. He was still a man.

Maybe wandering around the downtown area until I get mugged by a homeless person or the cops pick me up is my only option right now. There was a park nearby and he was sure the bums hung out and panhandled there. He'd fit right in.

The heat was also getting to him. This wasn't like Biloxi heat, where a nice gulf breeze could cool you off for short periods and it wasn't as humid.

He was angry at everything and everyone. He wished he had his phone because he'd call someone to vent.

Who would you call? Steve sighed. He had no real friends. Lots of acquaintances. People he knew because of Her.

Steve stopped short in front of the nondescript office building, where hours before he'd been banished and tossed on the street. Some piece of Kathrine's Empire where she reigned supreme. He had been thrown out by *Her*. Another fucking *Her* ruining his life.

He gave it a double middle finger salute, hoping Katherine and Jackson and everyone else who still met there could see it.

It wasn't enough.

Steve looked around for something to break. Maybe it would make him feel better.

There were people on the street. If he did something stupid, there'd be witnesses.

He didn't care.

Large potted plants flanked the doors to the building. They looked heavy. Maybe he could knock them over and dump the soil onto the sidewalk.

Lame, he thought.

He needed to be destructive. Let them know he was mad as Hell and he wasn't going to take it anymore.

Steve grabbed the potted plant with both hands, grinning when he found it not as heavy as he thought it would be.

He hefted it onto one shoulder. He was going to toss all caution and common sense out and do this.

"What do you think you're going to do with that?"

Steve was in a rage. He wanted to get past whoever was talking to him. If he had to go through the person, he would. He needed to create chaos. Break a window or smash in the door. See how far he could get inside before security kicked his ass and the cops came. Put them all to the test.

"Seriously, you look like an idiot. There are cameras inside and out. Besides the fact Gary, the head of security, used to play for the Oakland Raiders back in the day. Like, when they were in Los Angeles. Gary was the unofficial buffer between the gangs and the players. He's pretty nasty. He could break you in half while eating soup and not spill a drop. I do all my fucking up in the old Hidden Truth offices because there's no Gary there. See?"

Steve put the potted plant on the ground and stared at Cull.

A stunning red head walked out of the Jacksonville office behind Steve and made her way up the sidewalk like she owned the world. Those pants hugged every curve and glowed in the Florida sun like an alien blue star. She didn't turn around to give Cull a look at her face. Women like that never turned around. They knew exactly what they were doing. He wanted to leave Steve and try to get her attention, but unfortunately, that wasn't part of the plan for now.

"Let's take a ride," Cull said. "This is just a rented space for meetings and shit. It's not even the real Hidden Truth office where the gritty work gets done. It's where they move money around and that's where things are about to get interesting for both of us."

"I don't have enough gas."

Cull smiled. "I'll drive. I'm guessing they screwed you over. I was waiting for it to happen. You and me, kid, are going to figure this out together."

"Can you buy me a cheeseburger and a beer?" Steve asked, his hands still shaking.

CHAPTER 12

Julius Caesar Discovered Fountain of Youth and Found Alive in Dubai Last Friday

"It looks like a photograph of women's underwear," Steve said.

"It is, but there's more." Cull fumbled with the mouse sensor at the bottom of the laptop's keyboard. There was a hell of a lot more than women's underwear, but that wasn't what Cull needed to show the kid. He accidentally closed the picture of the panties on Marty's dresser. "Shit. Hold on."

Steve pulled open one of the duffle bags on the end of the bed and dug through his clothes. "Are you sure you got everything that was mine?"

"Everything that was yours and probably a few extras, too." Cull leaned close to the screen on the desk in front of him.

"How are you going to get my phone back? You said you'd get my phone back."

"I'll figure it out. Why won't the picture open again?"

"You need to close out that other window, so the program doesn't think it's still open. Then, click it again." Steve stood and looked through the vertical blinds. "Whose house is this?"

"Belongs to a couple from Ohio. They left two days ago."

"Are they friends of yours?"

Cull zoomed in on the frame to the top of Marty's dresser above the panties in the picture on the screen and then he waited for the pixilation to resolve. "Never met them."

"We broke in?"

"I used the same key the renters use when they come in."

"How do you know they're not coming back?"

Cull zoomed in again. "Because they live in Ohio and they left two days ago. The next renters come in on Friday, so we'll need to find you a different place after that. How do you clear this image up?"

Steve leaned around Cull at the desk which belonged to the couple from Ohio and worked through several menu options in rapid succession. "How do you doctor photos for your job, if you're this tech illiterate?"

"I know how to use my own computer and the ones at Hidden Truth with the Photoshop. You have a different photo program on your computer."

"Because Photoshop is as outdated as PowerPoint." Steve clicked a few more times. "What is it you want? The stuff on that piece of paper?"

"Yeah, that's it."

Steve clicked again and the image cleared enough for the string of numbers in a column down the crooked page to be legible. The paper bent on its top fold, hiding some of the sequences, but the rest were clear enough to show the bleed of black into the texture of the page itself.

"Perfect. Can you do a screenshot of that and send it to me?"

Steve sighed and pressed two buttons. The screen went white for an instant and a mock shutter click sounded. "Is that all you wanted? You're going to have security toss me out as soon as I send you an e-mail?"

"I prefer a text." Cull winked and clicked his tongue. "Don't be such a pussy. Katherine walks all over everyone."

"You seemed to get by okay?" Steve returned to the window and leaned his head on his forearm against the glass as he stared at the ocean.

"Yeah, I got fired. I just walked out and moved on, trusting something would work out. Not giving a shit looks a lot like winning sometimes."

"It worked out. Jackson tricked me into creating the app and then fucked me over but good."

"Time to make your own luck then."

Steve sighed. "So, what are those numbers? Bank accounts. You robbing someone?"

"I think they are and I think so," Cull said. "I was sort of looking for this or something like it when I went in."

"Whose house is that?"

"A couple from Ohio. They left two days ago. I told you that."

"Not this house. The house where you took your panty picture."

"Doesn't matter. A piece of shit stealing from more powerful pieces of shit about to be skimmed by us."

"Us?" Steve stepped away from the glass, rustling the blinds, but not facing Cull at the computer. "You want me to help with embezzlement? You're fucking crazier than you smell."

"Money is already stolen and hidden. We just need to take a little more from this stash and cover our tracks."

"I design apps. I don't rob banks."

"You drive drunk assholes home from the casinos. You made an app and the fuckers who fucked you over are the ones being fucked by this guy who is still drawing a healthy check from the people who stole your app out from under you and tossed you to the curb. Of course, if you think throwing a potted plant through a satellite office window for a global media empire is revenge enough, I could always drop you off there with all your stuff on that curb again."

"I make an app for Jackson and I steal from a criminal's bank account for you. Then, what? I get thrown out on my ass again. I've already played this game once, Cull. Fool me once, right?"

"You see how I handle computers. You could screw me, and I wouldn't know the first thing about how to stop you."

Steve stared at Cull. He glanced at the numbers on the screen and back at Cull. "Why are you involving me then?"

"Who else? Jackson? My ex? You take the payday you should have got from the app. and I'll take a cut, too. We'll siphon it through a couple accounts to make it hard to trace. Moving money, that I know about. We take what we want, but slowly, in small pieces. Anyone who comes looking and busts him will just think he spent what is missing. If he's caught, the trail will end there. See?"

"How much is in there?"

"We won't know until we open them up."

Steve shook his head. "Where are these accounts?"

"No idea." Cull tilted his head as he stared at the screen. "Well, I got some ideas, but I don't know. Some of these numbers are accounts and the others are passcodes. I know which sites might have been used once we figure out what is what."

"And I need to do this before Friday when the renters show up?"

"It would make getting you a better place easier. Sure."

"Is this Mob money?"

Cull laughed. "Jesus, is that Jackson talking again? He loves that story. I think he's starting to believe the bullshit we've been printing all these years."

"So, it's not true?"

Cull wrinkled his nose and squinted. "Well, it's kind of true. It's a legacy cost left over from Katherine's father running papers up in the Northeast before the *Hidden Truth* and any of us had a hair on our balls. It's not a day-to-day thing of concrete shoes or anything really. This money is not their money. Not really."

Steve said, "You're going to get me killed; I can feel it."

"But you're not saying no, right?" Cull tapped the screen.

"Don't get greasy fingerprints on my screen." Steve used the tail of his shirt to wipe off a smear from one of the numbers on the zoomed image. "How did you know about these accounts?"

Cull clicked his tongue. "I didn't know as much as suspected it for a while. I was digging around in...I was digging around. I thought this would be in a lockbox, so I didn't think to look right out in the open. If I considered the source, I should have suspected it though."

"Is it that Marty guy from the paper? The editor?"

Cull stood up and stepped away from the computer. "Don't worry about who it is. I got that text from Jackson which turned out to be your passcode. Then, it got me thinking. and I remembered the paper on the back of the dresser. I almost moved it when I put out the panty montage, but then didn't bother. It was enough for me to go back into the picture for a closer look."

"And now here we are." Steve sat down at the desk in the seat Cull had vacated, but didn't face the screen.

"Can you do it?" Cull crossed his arms and stared down at Steve.

Steve laughed, but then swallowed and stared back. "If you can give me an idea of where to start and your plan for covering our trail, so we don't end up with matching pairs of those legacy shoes in concrete, checks out, then maybe."

"Good. I think you'll be happy with the results. You get back at those who screwed you without them knowing. Best way to do it."

Steve frowned. "Why is that the best way?"

"Trust me. You dish out the pain and you're clear of the fallout. Take the payday tax free."

Steve lowered his eyes to the floor. "We'll see."

Cull's phone chimed and he took it out of his pocket. "That app is going like gangbusters."

"I don't want to think about it."

Cull clicked his tongue. "Money will roll in. Everyone will get drunk on it. The bastard will keep skimming and we'll skim the skimmer. This time you'll be in control and I'll be the one trusting you."

"What if I decide to screw you this time?"

"Wouldn't be the first and won't be the last. I'm counting on it being a better deal for you that we stick together on this at least." Cull put his phone away. "Jackson wants to meet about *Hidden Truth's* new deal for us. Apparently, we're going back on the road to check out the stories on the app. They're coming in so fast I don't know how that's supposed to work."

"They're going to kick off the premium memberships soon, I bet," Steve said. "People can hide stories about themselves and see special details on stories about other people. People will get a chance to confirm or deny stories. I guess that's what you will do."

"Great. Hopefully they won't fire us mid-trip this time."

"Yeah, tell Jackson I said to go fuck himself."

"Sure thing." Cull turned for the bedroom door.

"And find my phone."

"I'll try," he called from the hallway.

"You're sure no one is coming before Friday."

"I'm sure." Cull opened the front door. "Still, if someone besides me comes in, make a break for it. I'll check on you soon."

Cull closed the door before Steve could answer.

CHAPTER 13

My Father-in-Law Was Raised by Bigfoot

Fitzy ordered another Grande Chai tea latte, three pump, skim milk, lite water, no foam, extra hot and stood off to the side to wait for it.

He'd been crashing in this lame coffee shop for an hour, waiting for Melinda to show.

His phone was on the table and it buzzed again.

And again.

Fitzy sighed and turned the volume off. People kept glancing in his direction. Did they know who he was? Were they reading the bullshit lies Melinda had been posting this week?

Where was this fat bitch?

The barista glanced in his direction and waved him back to the counter. She pointed at his coffee cup without a word, as if she couldn't be bothered to actually hand it to him. He hated the shitty service in this fancy bullshit chain. The coffee was too strong, too expensive, and rarely made right. The people behind the counter were a bunch of illiterate kids who never spelled his name right.

FITZEE was written on the cup with a little heart at the end, as if that was supposed to make it alright.

He looked at the bitch who'd made his latte, but she was busy helping the long line of customers.

Melinda had called him Fitzee on the *Hidden Truth* app.

Everyone stared. When Fitzy turned to look directly at someone, they acted like they were deep in conversation with someone else or reading a book or looking at their phone. Suddenly,

everyone in the place was too busy to glance in his direction.
He was calling bullshit on all of this.

If Melinda didn't show in the next five minutes, he was going
back to work and maybe he'd start his own rumors about the
heifer.

Like the fact she stunk during sex. *I bet she didn't want anyone
to hear that. Or that she wasn't very good giving head. How about the
fact she dyed her fucking blonde hair?*

He smiled, sure the world would want to know all of her dark
secrets, too.

Why had he said a fucking word to the rhino-bitch?

It was bad enough he'd slept with her so many times in the
past few weeks. He could see she was falling in love with him,
but he'd been too nice to put her in her place. Her extra wide place.

Melinda had been a good time, but it wasn't worth this
bullshit. Fitzy knew he didn't deserve it.

He took a sip of his latte, which wasn't even right. At most it
was "two pump."

His phone lit up with an incoming call.

Finally. *The bitch is calling to give me a lame excuse why she couldn't
get out of work. She was probably too busy destroying a Chinese buffet.*

Fuck. Fitzy stared at the phone. It was Ian.

No way he was having this conversation today. *Or ever.*

Fitzy put his phone down and saw Melinda, with a big smile,
standing near the doorway. She had another fat chick with her.

He waved her over, not bothering to stand. He'd been a perfect gentleman when they'd first started dating. Holding her car
door. Standing when she got up from the dinner table. Being nice
and complimenting her.

"This is my friend, Sharon. She works with me. She's also
my witness," Melinda said and sat across from Fitzy. Her friend
pulled a chair out, nearly sitting at the next table, but staring at
Fitzy.

He didn't like the way she was staring, with a stifled grin on
her face and a sparkle in her eyes. The fat bitch was laughing at
him.

"Let's make this quick. Why did you want to see me? You

stopped returning my phone calls a week ago. I thought your last text, when you called me a fat ugly whore, would be the last time I'd see or hear from you," Melinda said and smiled. "I can't imagine what changed your mind."

"Take it down or else," Fitzy said.

"Or else what?"

"I'll tell the world your secrets. Call you and your fat ass out," Fitzy said.

"You're calling me a fat ass? You weigh, what…three-fifty? I'm a hundred and sixty pounds," she said.

"All fat."

Melinda and her friend both laughed.

"I'm not a Barbie, but I'm not heavy, asshole. Is that what this is about? You thought you were fucking the fat girl and you were afraid your buddies would look down on you?" Melinda threw her head back and laughed. Loudly. Everyone started to openly stare.

"Were you afraid Ian might be mad you were fucking a chick?" It was her annoying friend chiming in. Fitzy didn't need her shit. He didn't even know her. He was sure she was a fucking dyke. Probably a drug addict or she'd been abused as a child. Something which made her so fucked up she laughed at other peoples' expense.

"I need you to take down those lies." Fitzy wanted to throw his latte in her face, but he'd paid too much for it. Based on the looks from his coworkers and especially his boss, he knew he was likely to get fired. He didn't need to waste his drink.

Especially on these two fat dyke bitches.

His phone lit up again. He put his hand over it.

Her asshole friend started laughing. "Holy shit. It's his boyfriend calling. I saw Ian on the screen."

"Fuck off," Fitzy said way too loudly. Not that it mattered since all conversation in the place had stopped and everyone was openly staring.

"You mean fuck Ian. Right?" Melinda asked, smiling as she made sure everyone was staring at her fat face and had heard her bullshit.

"It's all lies." Fitzy stood, his chair hitting the floor.

"Nothing happened." He pointed at Melinda. "Fatty is mad because I stopped seeing her."

"Dude, you're the fat ass. She's got some curves, but in the right places," a smiling guy at the next table said and grinned at Melinda. "If you're done with this homo maybe I can take you out Friday night."

Fitzy threw his cup at the guy, but it missed, hitting the other side of the table and splashing harmlessly on the floor.

"He even throws like a girl," a woman said from somewhere in the room. It was followed by quite a few people laughing.

"Is Ian effeminate, too?"

"There's no shame in being gay, but don't talk shit about other gay people."

"If you ever admit and come out of the closet, there's a cool club near Riverside you should check out."

Melinda was smiling. Her friend was coming out of her seat she was so fucking happy.

Fitzy wanted to run and hide. "This is fucked up. You people are all fucked up. It didn't happen. She's a liar. How would she know, anyway?"

"You told her," the guy at the next table said. "I read the story on the app. Heck, man, we all read it. You're messed up sucking another dude off in the bathroom if you're swearing you're not gay."

"It's not gay. It's something I like to do," Fitzy said and covered his mouth. Why the fuck was he talking to these ingrates? They were a bunch of fuckups hanging out at a coffee shop in the middle of the day. None of them worked important jobs like he did.

A woman with obnoxiously red hair sat in the corner watching the whole scene with morbid glee. It was like she came here just for this moment. Maybe she did.

His phone buzzed again on the table. Out of reach.

Melinda picked it up and answered.

"Hello? Fitzy's phone." Melinda grinned and covered the phone, looking around. "It's Ian."

A few people cheered like they were at a sporting event.

"He sounds really pissed," Melinda said. The crowd erupted in clapping.

Fitzy sprung at Melinda, snatching the phone from her hand. He jabbed a finger in her face. "This isn't over."

She smiled. "You're over. Maybe next time, after you fuck a girl, you'll have the common decency to call her back. You'll also not admit you like cock in your mouth on a third date, too, *Fitzee*."

He knew the way she strung out his name she was mocking him. He'd told her about Ian spelling his name wrong the first time they'd met at the bar, where Ian was working and took his drink order.

Ian ran with a Florida branch of the Warlocks motorcycle club. He was a big, burly dude with half his body covered in tattoos.

"We need to talk," Ian shouted. Even without it pressed to his ear, Fitzy could hear the words and the anger. "Meet me at the park. Twenty minutes."

Melinda laughed. "Looks like your boyfriend is mad you pulled him from the closet."

"He's going to kill me," Fitzy said.

"I'm sure you'll kiss and make-up."

Fitzy shook his head. "He's in a fucking bike gang. He carries knives and a .357. When I say he's going to kill me, I literally mean he's going to shoot me. Dead. I'm a dead man, you fat bitch."

Melinda wasn't smiling anymore.

Fitzy stood and waved his hands in the air. "You people are animals. All of you. Getting off on the pain and secrets of others? You can all go fuck yourselves. Each and every one of you. I hope someone in your life, even someone who you hung out with briefly, decides to screw you over so badly someone wants to kill you."

"We should go," Melinda said to her friend.

"This is on you," Fitzy said. "All of you."

He pushed through the crowd, half of them still catcalling and laughing, and went to see Ian and hoped he was killed quickly.

CHAPTER 14

Mole People Blackmail Vegas Mob from Deep within the Earth

"Is this the driveway?" Jackson pointed across Cull's face at another decorative stone wall and gate.

The Chevelle rumbled under them and thumped twice, threatening to die. Jackson revved the engine and lurched past the driveway he pointed toward.

Cull pushed Jackson's hand away from his face. "I don't know. None of these houses have numbers and the neighborhood didn't have a sign out front. It's like these rich ass fuckers don't want to be found."

Jackson slid his phone down his thigh toward his knee. He spread his fingers to zoom in on the directions. "On the right…Italian marble and grey cobblestone…Jesus Christ …." He raised his eyes and followed the curve of the road between McMansions. "Yeah, these kinds of assholes figure if you belong here, then you'll know where you're going without signs or street numbers."

"I guess we don't belong here."

The car rumbled again.

Jackson said, "You sure you can afford to just give me this beauty. We're still just grunts on payroll at this point."

"Well, it's the least I could do."

"I've seen you do less."

Cull scratched his nose with an extended middle finger. "I spent my severance wisely before we were rehired again. If I need to put it up for another gambling binge, I'll let you know."

"Wisely? Does that mean this car and back child support?"

"Oh, that would have been smarter. I invested in blow, hookers, and bribing cops. I might need to borrow the keys when next month's payment comes up."

"Speaking of recent fuck overs, I haven't seen or heard from Steve. I guess he went back to Mississippi to try to win back his girl. I expected some royal freak-out or a shootout back at the offices, you know? It was good you weren't around for all that. The kid looked so heartbroken. I was surprised he was surprised actually."

"Guess he wasn't the type." Cull kept his eyes forward. "Is that Italian marble?"

"No, I think that's flagstone. Italian marble is pink. Usually. I think. And that's on the left. Directions say on the right."

"Maybe they expected us to make the loop through the neighborhood the other way."

Jackson stared at his phone on his knee. "I don't know."

"On the subject of fuck-ups, has Marty been back in?"

"I hadn't heard about him being fired, but that's what you asked Katherine for, wasn't it?" Jackson said.

"He hasn't been fired, but he hasn't been back in either."

Jackson glared at Cull. "How do you know he hasn't been fired?"

Cull chewed at the inside of his mouth. "I asked if I could have his office and someone told me. Just curious where he's been, if the paper is still running."

"He could have come back after we went on the road this time, so he wouldn't have to see us. Maybe the app is taking over everything for *Hidden Truth*, so he's getting transferred to the coupon circular."

Cull sniffed. "Yeah, he'd find a way to fuck that up too and lose the company millions in the process."

"Probably." Jackson made a turn and pulled into the vast driveway of a three-story house with a pink tiled face around and over the entryway. "I think this is it."

"This is not the typical neighborhood on wheels where we do most of our business."

"No, it's not."

Cull reached for his camera, but Jackson put a hand on his

forearm. "We're not taking any pictures. It's not that kind of assignment."

Cull shook his head. "If the guy won't confirm or deny, we're running the story and we'll need pictures."

Jackson opened the door. "We're not supposed to bring in a camera. That was the deal."

Cull opened his door and spit on the pristine driveway. "Lock the doors. I don't want my camera stolen while I'm not doing my job."

Jackson laughed and locked the driver's door. "Yeah, not that kind of neighborhood and not that kind of car. You'll need to lock your own door."

Cull patted his pocket. "I'm bringing my phone and if this executive piece of shit re-negs, I'm taking a camera phone pic like some silly college bitch."

"Whatever suits you."

The door opened before they finished climbing the steps. A mountain of a man in a dark suit and sunglasses waved them forward. He closed the door and patted them down. The man took their phones and then pushed them forward. They passed under a large chandelier into a broad hallway. The man pushed them through an entry on the left.

An older, skinny gentleman in a grey suit stood in front of a desk. The walls were lined with built-in bookshelves full of leather-bound tomes.

Jackson said, "We're here to see…."

The man held up a hand. "Do not speak. Not a word. Not either of you."

Cull took a step toward the couch.

"Don't sit down either." The man placed a locked, silver briefcase on the floor with the handle up between them. "This is it. All of it. Locked. It won't be opened before you deliver it. The details are already arranged. Don't speak about this to anyone. Take it and leave now."

"We were supposed to speak directly to…." Jackson stopped talking without being prompted.

The man tapped the case with his toe, causing it to wobble. "This house belongs to no one connected to anyone you know.

Your being here will mean nothing to no one. So, go away and crawl back into the hole you live in between the times you crawl out for other people's dirty work."

"How do we know this isn't some kind of bomb, if we don't open it?" Cull said.

"The reason I asked you not to speak was because I didn't want to hear you idiots talk." The man stared a moment. "So, shut up, stupid. Get out of here before I have him throw you out."

Jackson took the case by the handle and they left the house. The mountain of a bodyguard handed back their phones and closed the door behind them. The case went into the trunk and then Jackson drove them out of the neighborhood which had no signs or addresses.

"Virginia is lovely this time of year, don't you think?" Cull asked.

Jackson laughed as he scrolled through his phone on his leg as he drove. "Yeah, nice people. Hear it's for lovers."

"Someone sure got fucked today. Maybe we should blow off these other meetings and get this mystery case back down to Florida as quick as we can."

"It's just money," Jackson said. "A lot of it, sure, but just hush money. I mean, diamond level membership."

"Oh?" Cull rubbed his forehead and closed his eyes. "We are offering a level above platinum now? Is that Katherine's idea?"

"Who the hell knows? Probably. She has an army of programmers in three different countries handling that sort of stuff now. I think diamond memberships are for really rich and powerful and famous people who don't want their really bad secrets coming out."

"Yeah, I bet we have a bomb in our trunk."

Jackson shook his head. "They know that no one important is coming to pick up the membership payment. Same as that guy and that house are technically no one important to our Diamond Level Senator friend there. We're fine."

Cull laughed. "So, you're saying we should be okay because we aren't important enough to blow up?"

"Exactly."

Cull shook his head. "Someday, you'll eat those words and I'll probably be right next to you, cutting and chewing, too." Cull's phone chirped a couple of times. He took it and groaned. "We're never going to keep up with confirming all these stories. A bunch of them aren't even in this country."

"We're not confirming all of them in person."

"And you need to show me how to turn off these notifications on my phone. They never stop day or night."

"I'll have to do it later. We're at the next place."

They pulled onto a trail covered in pine straw and followed the winding drive up behind a rusty camper. Weeds grew between the boards of the porch. The wood plank house was stained almost red except where black spots spread up from the ground out of deeper piles of pine straw. The roof cut at such a severe slope that the house looked like a spike stabbing up, out of the forest, at the sky.

"I'm bringing my camera this time," Cull said. "This is not a nice neighborhood."

"It's quiet." Jackson opened his door. "But no one here is buying diamond memberships today."

"Then, why are we here?" Cull slammed the car door with the hand not clutching the camera. The impact echoed in an odd crisscross between trees which did not strike Cull as natural.

"If he confirms the story, then it bumps up into the paid levels and not everyone in the world can see it."

They crunched over the brown straw toward the sagging board steps of the porch.

"Tricky."

"Yeah, that's why we don't have to go in person every time. More and more people are calling into Katherine's phone-banks in India. They can't wait to prove they are guilty, just so their mothers and bosses don't find out."

Cull followed Jackson up the steps. "Of course, more and more of those people are getting paid memberships to see the really juicy stories, right?"

"God bless America." Jackson knocked on the door through the frame of an outer metal door missing its screen. "Time to upgrade to platinum or diamond, if your secrets are that bad."

"Mine are that bad, but no one gives enough of a shit to report me."

Jackson winked. "Or to put a bomb in your truck."

Cull shook his head. "Going to eat those words."

The door opened and Cull moved his camera hand behind his back. The guy who answered wore no shirt or shoes. He had the tattoo of an eagle faded to dull greenish-blue in the center of his chest. An old surgical scar rose from the waistband of his grey sweatpants above his right hip. His dark hair hung greasy around his eyes and stuck up in wild strands from the back. The unruly spikes reminded Cull of the severe spike of the house's roof.

Everything stabbing up at whoever might be above?

The man moved his right hand behind his back just like Cull.

"Are you Bradley Sholes?"

Bradley turned his eyes onto Jackson. "Are you press? Are you more assholes looking for justice for shit that don't matter and can't be fixed?"

"We're from *Hidden Truth*," Jackson said. "Wanted to see if we might be able to help you put this mess behind you. We can talk about what happened and then not everyone will see the story anymore."

"You motherfuckers." Bradley's eyes glazed over and he laughed. "You're a little late to fix this shit now."

"We can step outside," Jackson said. "This can be handled in private where your wife and daughter won't hear any of it."

"They already know everything." Bradley pushed open the metal door. "Come on in. We can talk about this all together. Make it right, like you said."

Jackson took a step onto the threshold, but Cull put a hand on his arm and stopped him. He thought about Jackson stopping him from bringing the camera into their last stop. "We need to get some paperwork from the car. We'll be right back."

Jackson met eyes with Cull. He stared a moment, but then Jackson's eyes widened. "Sure. Sorry. I should have brought it. We'll just get it and meet you inside, Bradley."

They stepped back from the door. Bradley brought the

handgun around from behind his back.

Jackson and Cull leapt from the porch without touching the steps. Bradley took dead aim on them, but didn't fire.

Cull lifted his camera and snapped pictures as they ran. The muscles on Bradley's gun hand tightened and released over and over, but no bullets fired and the gun didn't click like it was empty either.

Bradley lowered the gun. "Fuck me. I should have saved a few bullets for you two, if only I knew you were coming. Once I started shooting her, I just couldn't stop. As soon as she said she was leaving with my daughter, I just couldn't stop. But she jumped in front of her mother and the first one went through them both. I couldn't stop. Give me a minute, you assholes, and I'll reload real quick. We'll make this shit right."

His voice echoed in that unnatural crisscross.

The Chevelle acted as if it wouldn't start, but then turned over. Jackson ground it into reverse and spun the tires on the straw. The backend weaved toward the trees on both sides over and over as they barreled backward toward the main road.

"What the fuck did he do?" Cull snapped photos of the house with Bradley still on the porch.

Jackson watched through the back window of the car as the street came into view. "He killed his wife and daughter before we got here, I guess. We need to get out of here before the police come and find a briefcase of money in our car at a murder scene."

"No, I mean what did he do that got him on the app?"

Jackson backed onto the pavement and shifted into the drive. The car roared forward down the center line before Jackson finally found his lane. "People said he raped some girl in high school. The girl got pregnant and moved one town over. The kid is grown now and never knew. Well, until now. Two other girls from college made accusations after the first rape was reported. Other folks posted he was sleeping with a secretary at his construction company. Stuff was piling up real Bill Cosby style, so that's why we got sent."

"He really got 'hashtag MeToo-ed,' didn't he? The murders should distract from that now." Cull's phone chirped again. According to some news site, another lawsuit was filed against

Hidden Truth, but the app was registered on some island and was legally separate from the magazine. Katherine's lawyers claimed to be as upset about the app as everyone else, but it was out of their control. There was more to the article, but Cull didn't open it. "Yeah, looks like it piled up. You want to make our other meetings or you want to get back to Florida and let Katherine get a jump on laundering this bomb in our trunk?"

Jackson didn't answer and they continued on through Virginia with the uneven sound of the engine for a few miles.

CHAPTER 15

All the Gold in Fort Knox Was Stolen by Ancient Aliens!

Steve decided he was going to buy a motorcycle when the money cleared. A big, bad-ass Harley. He'd ride into Biloxi in style.

Just a few more minutes, he thought. He'd made the deal with Cull so the money wouldn't start moving right away and might be traced.

To anyone looking, it was an offshore account that had been retro-dated three years previous with no movement, which would raise no red flags.

He'd been living off of the thousand Cull had given him a couple weeks back. It had been more than enough to get a decent hotel room right on the sand in Daytona Beach and eat at the best spots in town.

The siphoning of the money was now on autopilot. No way Katherine's new techno geek squad would even know it was missing. Steve had made sure of it, with so many false firewalls and encryption, as soon as the numbers were input into the system, it would make Alan Greenspan spin in his grave. *Was that dude dead?* Steve couldn't remember. He wasn't even positive what the guy really did other than he was an important money guy Steve's father always used to talk about.

Cull had wanted Steve to make sure every single thing he could do was done, even to the point of overkill.

Six more minutes.

Steve had about a hundred dollars left in cash. He'd need to go to the bank and withdraw a few hundred more. Fewer than five bills. Enough to get him through the week, but not enough to stir up suspicion.

All from the comfort of his phone while sitting on the beach watching the local chicks in bikinis. If it wasn't for the fact that he wanted to get back to Biloxi soon and stick his wealth in everyone's face, he might be inclined to stay right in this spot. Maybe buy the hotel itself.

Tonight, he'd head to Hooters and then the mall to buy some new clothes. Fancy things. He'd need an outfit to wear on the motorcycle. There was a huge Harley dealership around here somewhere. He'd need to check it out and test-ride a bike, too.

Two minutes.

Steve stared at two women sitting together on a blanket and talking, up the beach from him. From this distance, he didn't know if they were hot or even young. He wondered how much cash he would need to give them to make out in front of him.

Not that he would ever do it, but it was a cool fantasy. The rich guy, wandering around the casino or the bar, handing out crisp hundred-dollar bills and getting women to go down on each other for his own amusement.

He might get a hooker tonight, too, but not one of these skanky Daytona Beach ones he kept seeing up the road. They'd made a movie about one of them killing johns years ago. From the looks of the prostitutes walking the streets today, they weren't too far behind.

Showtime. Steve clapped his hands and picked up his phone, logging in as he stood. He would wander back to his room, take a big shit, and get dressed.

When he logged in, he was confused at first.

Instead of the roughly fifty grand that should be in the account, it was less than eight.

Seven-thousand three-hundred and fifteen dollars.

"Shit." Steve went to his hotel room. Maybe he'd fucked up and the money wasn't pulling correctly. Maybe these new techs had changed something he hadn't foreseen and the money had stopped.

Maybe…fucking Cull.

Steve saw the transactions. Five days ago, he'd pulled two

grand from the account in Orange Park. Three days ago, it was twenty large. Yesterday, he'd taken thirty thousand dollars and deposited it into his own bank account.

Steve hacked into Cull's account and saw the money had been taken out this morning. The account had thirty-seven cents in it.

He stared at the number in Cull's account before closing the tab and going back to their joint account. The secret account no one was supposed to know about because they were supposed to have been smart and not touched it for two weeks.

Two lousy fucking weeks and then they could pull twenty-five thousand each out and no one would be any wiser.

But they were. All because of Cull.

Steve wanted to kill Cull, that backstabbing motherfucker. More than he wanted to kill Jackson even.

His hands were shaking as he dialed, expecting Cull to ignore his calls.

Cull answered on the fourth ring.

"What did you do?" Steve asked through gritted teeth. He paced back and forth in his hotel room, out onto the balcony and across to the front door and out into the parking lot and back.

"I don't even get a hello, kid?"

"You took the money. You took the money. You took the money."

Cull chuckled. "You're repeating yourself. You all right? And I didn't take all of it. I left you a bunch. I didn't even touch the account the last three days so there should be plenty of moolah in there for you."

"There isn't. You know why? Because they froze the account. The money still there is useless. When they caught us and found the account, you know what they did? They left the money so we'd think it was still there. That way they could trace you the next time you went into the account. They saw you do it. They saw me try to do it just now. We're royally fucked." Steve stopped walking.

He needed to pack and get out of town.

"My bad," Cull said. He sounded anything but sincere.

"We're going to prison. For a long time."

"Nah. No way they know who took it. Didn't you put in safeguards for that kinda shit?"

Steve groaned. "Yes. The best safeguard was not touching the account. Logging into it. Doing anything to let anyone know it was even there." He punched the air with his free hand. "This is my fault. I trusted you."

"Yeah, I have to agree. That was your first mistake. Can I call you back? I need to bet on the next race," Cull said.

"You're gambling the money away? That's why you're in Orange Park. I'm guessing it's a racetrack."

Cull snorted. "Everyone knows betting on the horses is stupid. I stopped that years ago. I'm at the dog track. I was on a roll a couple of days ago. I missed an exacta by one damn dog. Can you believe it?"

"I know what you're trying to do."

"You do?" Cull asked.

"You're trying to confuse me. Change the subject. It won't work. You really screwed us over by taking the money."

"I'm sorry. I thought I had a sure thing. It couldn't wait. I didn't see a reason to wait to take the money out. You didn't tell me how important it was to keep it in the account."

Steve groaned again. "Sure as shit, I did. It was the first thing and the last thing I told you. Under no circumstances touch the money until today at noon. I even had you repeat it back to me. Say the date and time three times. I'm not sure what part you missed."

"Obviously the part where I could take the money out early. I needed it. I've been on the road with Jackson on and off since this app blew up. I needed to unwind. Besides, I swear I was going to replace it. I figured I'd make an extra chunk of change on the side. You wouldn't care. If you did, I'd cut you in for a few bucks." Cull was drowned out by an announcement about the next race about to start.

"I'm turning myself in. I can't be on the run. I have no money left," Steve said. "You fucked me."

"Just stay cool. We'll figure this out together."

"You expect me to trust you?"

"You don't really have a choice. I screwed up. I'm sorry. I said it again. I never did that in any of my marriages. We'll put the money back into the account. I have it on me, but no idea how to do it. Drive up to Orange Park and we'll work this out," Cull said. "Hold on a sec, Steve. Yeah, hey, put a sawbuck on Captain Nemo in the third."

"Stop gambling the money away."

"I got a good feeling on this one. Besides, I have enough in my pocket to cover what I took out. I will with this win, anyway. Get your ass up here so we can straighten it out," Cull said.

"We can't put the money back. It's too late for that. The account's been flagged. They know where you were and where I am now. We need to ditch our phones and leave town." Steve began pulling his clothes from the drawers.

"We need to sit still. You know how people get caught? They run. I saw that line in a movie the other night. Maybe a TV show. Anyway, we need to be cool as the other side of the pillow."

"Did you hear that line in a movie, too?" Steve asked.

"Maybe."

"If I call Katherine and beg her not to press charges, what do you think she'll say?" Steve stuffed everything he owned into a garbage bag. He still had a week left on the room, but couldn't chance staying and being found.

"Katherine will get her crime friends to break our legs. We'll be swimming with the fishes off Jax Beach. Do *not* call her. That bitch can't be trusted. Look what she did to you." Cull groaned and Steve heard the crowd cheering in the background. "So damn close. Ugh."

"What about Jackson? Maybe I'll call him. I really don't trust you. I've also seen a lot of movies. I drive to Orange Park and you meet me in the bathroom and fill me with lead." Steve went into the bathroom and cleaned up his stuff.

"If you involve Jackson, you know what he'll do. He'll call Katherine. While I love the guy like a brother, he's another one you need to be wary of. He has his own agenda. The only person you can trust right now is me." Cull sighed. "Look, Kid, we can work through this. I'll see you soon?"

"I'm leaving in a couple of minutes. Give me the address so I can GPS it."

"Hey, Steve, mind bringing me a cup of coffee, too? The java at the track is awful."

"Sure. Anything else? Need me to buy you lunch even though I'm broke?"

Cull laughed. "Just coffee. I'm not an asshole." He disconnected.

Steve went to the parking lot and stopped. A black sedan was parked at the entrance to the hotel. It could be someone checking in, but he didn't want to take a chance.

He imagined mobsters inside working over the desk clerk to find out which room he was staying in.

Cull couldn't be trusted. Neither could Katherine or Jackson.

Steve turned and cut through the pool area and back to the beach. He'd walk a few blocks and find a bus or a taxi. He needed to get far away from Daytona Beach and close enough to Jacksonville right now.

Figure out what needed to be done.

As he stumbled through the sand, carrying all of his possessions in a black garbage bag, Steve wondered how he'd dropped this far and how he hadn't realized back in Biloxi there was still a precipice to fall off of.

By the time he got to the next break and crossed the street to a fast food restaurant, he knew what he had to do and who he could call. Luckily, he'd managed to download all manner of information from Cull, Jackson, and *The Hidden Truth*.

Steve called Marty.

CHAPTER 16

Ninja Kill-Squads Kidnapping Women and Children Right Out of Their Hotel Rooms

Jackson raised his hands over the table. "You called me. So, what do you want to do?"

The young woman across from him stared back. Green eyes. Chestnut hair in what Jackson thought was called a pixie cut. She had on a spaghetti strap top which sagged enough for him to tell she wasn't wearing a bra. She was perky enough to get away with it. Those couldn't be real. Real life couldn't be that great.

Cull always said, *If you can touch them, they are real.*

She said nothing, and the rims of her eyes gathered moisture. Even with the distraction of her perkiness and the numb haze of years of tabloid "journalism," he felt a tug of guilt for what this girl was going through. It wasn't even about her this time. It was her husband's shit she was here trying to clean up.

Dude should have come to handle it himself. Why was this her problem anyway? Jackson looked away from her wet eyes. It was because of him. He had championed the app and used it to railroad his way back into a steady paycheck.

A man in swim trunks sat on a wicker stool by the bar. The mirror behind the bottles reflected the lights around the room too brightly. Metallic pings and electronic squawking from the arcade at the far end of the booths rang off the wet tile from families walking through from the pool.

A dude sat three booths closer to the pool behind Jackson with his back to him. He wore a pink Panama City shirt with the sleeves cut off and hunched over a red basket with a burger and steak cut fries on checkered paper.

Who wore a shirt for a different Florida city on their vacation?

The bartender raised his eyebrows and lifted an order pad in Jackson's direction. Jackson waved him off and turned his attention back to her. The bright sand leading to the ocean made the shadows in the resort bar grow deeper.

Her fists balled in front of her on the table in a way that seemed more desperate than angry. Her pixie cut didn't hide the rashy splotches on her cheeks the way she probably wanted as she bowed her head away from his gaze.

He kind of wished he was back in Nashville, researching and writing elaborate conspiracy theories for housewives going off their meds. He probably drove a few of them to divorce as they tried to convince their husbands to move them to Colorado to avoid super waves. Maybe a couple committed suicide, as they read about the coming judgement of God in fiery death from the sky and their trashy romance paperbacks. He didn't have to meet them in hotel bars and look into their sad faces when he worked there.

If Jackson was honest, he really wished he hadn't been busted on graduation night and gone to jail for a few months. He wouldn't have fucked away an entry level position to a real paper straight out of college then. He would have never ended up here watching this bitch cry over whatever it was her husband was called out for on the *Hidden Truth* app. He couldn't even remember what the hell it was the man did. It all blurred together now.

He couldn't remember her name. Maybe she'd let him call her Perky Pixie.

Jackson stared at smooth white skin which should have been covered by Mrs. Pixie's bra – maybe something lacey. It made him feel better about all the other things he didn't care to think about.

She looked up at him, but didn't meet his eyes. He wasn't looking at her face anyway. Her hands wrung instead of clinched. "Maybe we can work something out. I don't have enough for a room, but if you got one, maybe I could come up.

Maybe we could figure out what it takes to make everything right."

Jackson swallowed. He wished he wasn't staring at her tits when Perky said that. And he was glad he hadn't made Cull come along. If Cull didn't have the car with him, at least the asshole couldn't gamble it away this time.

"You shouldn't say things like that. You're far too much to turn down on that kind of bad idea."

"Then, let's see what we can do for each other. Okay?"

Eyes dropped back down with hands still wringing. The rashy red traveled down from Perky Pixie's neck and threatened the porcelain white of her breasts.

Jackson brought his gaze up to a gnarled, yellow strip of sticky paper dangling from the ceiling two booths closer to the ocean and about two dozen flies past needing to be changed. "None of the great stuff I'm sure you can do up there will change what we can agree to down here. None of this really has anything to do with me. Your...man just needs to either confirm or deny the stories. That decides what goes on the site and at what level of access."

"What about the 'rich dude' deal?"

Jackson looked into her green eyes. They were dry and narrowed now. The flush in her skin faded and her hands went flat and still on the table. "What do you mean?"

"Rich dudes get their shit hidden on the site. How do we get that deal?"

"The gold and platinum memberships are for sale to anyone. You just pay and you get to see the top-level stuff. No deal hides your profile – your husband's profile, I mean – from everyone. Either provide evidence the stories aren't true or confirm them. That's all we can do. I'm sorry."

"Just give us a platinum membership then and I'll give you platinum level service for it."

"I got no power over that. The company isn't going to let me screw with their money. Or screw for their money in this case, I guess. That would be suicide for both of us. Believe me."

Fists balled again, and knuckles went white. Pixie's jaw

clenched under the curve of her locks. "Let's just go up to a room and we'll work it out. Okay?"

"There's nothing to work out unless you find someone way more important than me to bang. Sorry we wasted each other's time."

Jackson stood and her eyes went wide. He paused and waited to see if she planned to burst into tears. He wondered if Perky Pixie could cry hard enough to make them bounce. She looked at the bartender instead.

The cord came down over his head and pulled Jackson away from the booth backward by his neck. He clawed at his throat as the man dragged him over the wet tile. Jackson saw the pink Panama City shirt and the unshaven man's teeth. The whirls and clangs from the arcade warbled and echoed in his skull. The closing black tunnel washed into his vision a lot faster than he expected.

Shit, he wished Cull was here.

The bartender slammed into the side of the Panama City shirt. Mr. Pink released the cord and shoved the bartender backward by his face.

Jackson sucked air in rough and wet. His vision faded back into light and color. He watched the man in swimming trunks and blue flipflops run toward the arcade, the pool, and the parking lot. Jackson's arms and legs felt watery and heavy. For a second, he couldn't remember why he was on the floor.

The woman drew her tennis shoe back and kicked Jackson in the ribs. Her laces were untied and she didn't have on socks. She drew back and kicked him again. Her breasts bounced with the impacts and almost escaped her top. Her tight shorts held everything else in place and he imagined what she might really be like in bed.

The pain brought Jackson into his head quicker.

"Get out of here right now. I'm calling the cops." The bartender came back in and Mr. Pink punched him hard enough to ripple the bartender's jowls. Pink still had the cord wrapped around his fist.

The bartender took out his cell phone as Jackson pulled himself up to his feet by the back of a booth. He looked down on the untouched burger and fat fries with the skins still on. The salt stood out in sharp crystals from the bright light slicing in from the ocean.

Perky Pixie beat her fists against his back. Jackson gave one wild, open-hand swing without looking. He backhand slapped her across the tits with a loud crack and she gasped. Definitely store bought.

The cord looped over his throat again, but Jackson got a hand between his skin and the line this time. Mr. Pink walked Jackson backward toward the arcade and pool exit.

The bartender had his phone up, but was filming instead of calling anyone. Pixie stepped between Jackson and the phone.

The guy jerked his weight sideways and hurled Jackson to the tile again. Jackson pumped his feet and clawed with the hand not trapped in the cord, but he couldn't get to standing again as he felt the spaces between tiles pull at his clothes as he went.

Jackson rolled over to his knees and stared at the cargo shorts and hiking boots walking backward. *What a dipshit!*

As Jackson flipped over to get dragged along on his knees, the cord twisted tighter and the blackness closed in again.

Jackson got one foot under him and launched himself forward. He planted a forearm into the inside of Mr. Pink's left knee and bent it out sideways with a brittle crack. The guy screamed high and shrill. He let go of the cord and slammed into the coin machine before hitting the blue carpet inside the arcade.

A few kids looked up as Jackson used the seat of a racing game to pull himself to his feet. He coughed hard twice and tasted blood.

She clawed at his face with both hands. One of her nails raked over his closed eyelid and Jackson saw a flash of red and green behind the lid. He jabbed his thumb into her throat. She gagged and let go with one hand, but left her nails dug into his cheek with the other.

Jackson growled and swung a hard, right hook for her cheek. He pictured one of her green eyes swelled shut and him sitting in lock-up with her husband. She staggered backward away from him and his closed fist hooked through empty air where her face used to be.

Mr. Pink banged the back of his head against the arcade carpet twice and screamed with his mouth wide open. The dude gripped his thigh with both hands just above his knee where his leg bent the wrong way. Jackson felt the urge to either spit in the guy's mouth or kick him in his bad knee.

Jackson felt a wave of dizziness wash through him and he turned away from Mr. Pink on the blue floor.

Jackson hobbled along and blasted through the crash bar into the pool area. The glass bounced off the trashcan with a bass note thump. He ran past the deck chairs and the staring eyes. He hit the metal gate with his hands shaking. It took him five tries to unlatch it and then he ran along the sidewalk across the fronts of parked cars.

He reached the one Cull had bought him and fumbled for the key.

She hit him from the side and he felt the metal bite hard into his ribs. The keys dropped onto the hood. Jackson grappled with her on the sidewalk until he got hold of the wrist of her knife hand in both of his hands. She pulled his hair and sunk her teeth into his forearm.

Jackson pushed her backward toward the textured side of the hotel. The bushes scratched at their legs and then her back slammed the wall. She did not let go of the knife nor her grip with her teeth.

He pulled her away from the wall and then slammed her three more times. On the third impact, he saw the knife was a butter knife from the hotel bar and restaurant. She dropped the knife in the bushes. Her head bounced and she let go with her teeth.

Jackson cupped the side of her face with both hands. Her hair was soft and cold. Why cold? He shoved her sideways into the opening for the stairs.

He checked his side as he stepped out of the bushes. His clothes weren't torn and he wasn't bleeding. At least not from his side where she tried to stab him.

He snatched up the keys and they jingled in his quaking

hands as he unlocked the door. He got the engine started and backed up until he hit the bumper of another car. He shifted into drive and raced out of the parking lot without looking.

Jackson fought his phone free of his pocket as he drove and scrolled for Cull's number. He could feel his pulse behind his eyes.

Before he could select the number, Cull called him, and he answered. "Jesus Christ, Cull ...."

"Listen, I've been trying to call you," Cull said. "We're in big fucking trouble right now."

"You have no idea."

"Drive out to the racetrack in Orange Park to get me right now. I'm leaving and going to wait for you somewhere nearby. I'll call you to let you know where in a few minutes. Just come on now. Don't stop for anyone or anything. No side trips. Get here now."

Jackson lifted his chin to look at the red irritation of the skin. A few purple divots marked the track along the path of the cord. Raw scratches down both cheeks lifted in ridges from his skin and welled with spots of blood. Somehow, he had lighter scratches vertically on his throat too. He didn't remember Perky Pixie getting her claws into his throat, but who the hell knew after all that nightmare?

If she and her husband, Mr. Pink, had lured him out of the restaurant on the pretense of getting laid, they probably would have choked him to death in one of the stairwells before anyone could intervene. Not even a shitty bartender more interested in recording than calling 9-1-1. Maybe they intended to choke him out and hold him hostage in a trunk.

It hurt when he swallowed.

"Cull, we may need to see if we can get our information and personal details off the...Cull, are you there?"

He took the phone away from his face to see the call had ended.

He had skin under his fingernails. Jackson didn't remember clawing anyone either. The dude's knee was the only good shot Jackson got in through the whole ordeal. Remembering the sound of that break made him queasy.

A pop-up on the screen showed he had missed two other calls from Cull and a call from Marty. Neither of them had left messages. "Fuck Marty."

Jackson tossed the phone onto the seat and drove toward Cull.

CHAPTER 17

Super Bowl Halftime Toilet Flushes Have Knocked the Earth Off Its Axis

Marty stared at the untouched drink on the counter and sighed. "Why me?"

Steve slapped the bar with his hands. "Who else could I turn to?"

"That's rich. If you think I'm your best choice to get your shit back together, you're in worse trouble than I thought. In fact, Buddy…you're royally fucked."

"I know you've been screwed over, too." Steve put a hand on Marty's shoulder. "Drink up. I saw the pictures."

"Pictures? What are you talking about?" Marty fucking knew. He also knew who'd taken them and why. Payback. Blackmail. Revenge. An ace in the pocket. Call it what you wanted, but he knew Cull had him by the balls.

"We can take them down."

Marty picked up the drink. Licked his lips. "Take down what exactly?"

"Cull. Jackson. Katherine. The *Hidden Truth* app."

Marty sniffed the drink. "What is this?"

Steve smiled. "The good stuff. Pappy Van Winkle bourbon. Fifty bucks a glass and that's cheap."

Marty put the glass down. "Is it poisoned?"

Steve frowned. "Why would I try to kill you? I need your help. And if I was going to do it, I'm not wasting my last ten to do it. You'd get whatever beer was a special during happy hour."

"You taste it first." Marty pushed the glass toward Steve. He didn't really think the guy was trying to kill him, but maybe he'd crushed some sleeping pills in the drink when Marty wasn't looking. Until recently this guy had been in cahoots with Cull and Jackson.

"Fine. But I'm drinking half of it." Steve took a big sip and grimaced. He put the glass down and his hands went to his throat as he began to cough.

Marty jumped off of his barstool.

Steve started to laugh and slapped the bar. "Gotcha. Seriously, you should've seen your face."

"Asshole." Marty finished the drink.

"I do have a couple of venereal diseases, though. You probably shouldn't have had a drink from that glass." Steve put up his hands. "I'm kidding. Lighten up."

"It's hard to lighten up when everything I've worked so hard for is now gone. This fucking app has killed my career. I'm bleeding cash. Your two buddies have made sure I have no power anymore. I knew I should've gone over Katherine's head and fired them when I had the chance." Marty held up the empty glass for the bartender to see.

"I'm not buying you another one," Steve said.

"I have enough for one more," Marty said. He was trying to joke, but it wasn't far from the truth.

The Hidden Truth, he thought sourly.

"I have a plan. I think. Hear me out and tell me if it makes sense to you. I worked on it on the way here, so it's in the infant stages," Steve said.

The bartender brought him another glass and Marty stared at it, watching the liquid move ever so slightly as someone tapped the bar or put their own drink down.

Maybe becoming a really good alcoholic will work for me, Marty thought. He doubted another paycheck was going to be deposited in his bank account, although he'd been pleasantly surprised last Friday. He was still technically on payroll, but his passkeys no longer worked. He could get into the lobby and hang out with the cleaning crew.

Since they hadn't fired him, he wondered if he could get another job. He vaguely remembered signing a confidentiality agreement a long time ago. He wondered what it covered and how screwed he was now.

At some point, the money would stop. They'd realize it was a clerical error cutting him checks or Katherine would decide he wasn't even worth hush money.

The more Marty thought about it the more he was sure he needed to do something, even if it was desperate and fool-hardy. He had nothing else.

Steve was still talking.

"What do you propose we do about it?" Marty asked.

"We take down the app. Haven't you been listening to me?"

Marty shook his head. "I tuned you out the last twenty minutes or so. Right after I got my second drink. Too busy worrying about my future and realizing I no longer had one."

"Can I get a soda, please?"

"Did you know I was editor of not only my high school but my college papers? I won awards." Marty smiled. "I had a bookcase with the top shelf filled with them."

"I think I saw it in the background of the pictures," Steve said. "I really trusted Cull and Jackson. Especially Jackson. He suckered me into working for free and Cull got me to steal the money and then took it right out from under me."

Marty stopped thinking about what could've been and had been and put his hand up. "Wait…say that last part again?"

"Shit."

"That's not what you said. You and Cull stole their money? What do you need me for?"

Steve sighed. "Cull took it and their tech team was alerted. I'm sure they're after me right now."

Marty looked around the bar. "You might have led them to me, you asshole?"

"I don't think I was followed."

"Suddenly you're an FBI agent? You can tell when you're being tailed?" Marty stood. "I'm going to the bathroom. Slipping out the back door. You count to twenty and walk out the front. I'll meet you three doors down."

"What store?"

"I have no idea. Count three fucking doors. Can you do that, Steve?"

Thankfully, he nodded.

Marty walked as if he was going to the bathroom. He was trying to act casual.

Two women in smart pant suits were at a table and they glanced in his direction as he passed. Were they spies? Sent by Katherine or the law?

A busboy carrying a full tray of dirty glasses and dishes passed Marty. Did he have a gun tucked in his waistband?

Fucking idiot. Stop watching bad Tom Cruise movies and get your head together, he thought.

The hall to the bathroom led only to the bathrooms. No exit. He opened the bathroom door. It had no window.

Steve was just getting up when Marty sat back down.

"We're trapped?" Steve asked.

"New plan. I leave through the front door and you count to twenty again. We meet tonight in the park across from *The Hidden Truth* building. Bring a bottle of anything and a glazed donut. To go." Marty took another look around. The two women in the corner were supposedly in a conversation, but maybe one of them had a listening device in her purse aimed at them. It wasn't safe to be talking out in the open.

"What time?"

Marty frowned. "What?"

"You just said tonight. Does that mean after six or closer to midnight? When you say a bottle of anything, do you mean alcohol? I told you I was broke, right? I can't even afford the glazed doughnut."

"Holy shit. You're not joking around." Marty wanted to slap the kid. They needed to get out of the bar and Steve was holding them up. "Meet me at eight. Eastern Standard Time. Directly in front of the doors, but in the park itself. Can you handle it?"

"I'm not an idiot."

Marty laughed. "You came to me for help. You're not the sharpest crayon in the box."

I have until tonight to figure out what needs to be done. Maybe Steve will get some thoughts as well. This is going to be a nightmare.

Marty walked out into the sunlight.

He noticed the two police cars and the officers a second before he saw Katherine. She was smiling. The cops weren't.

"Hey, Marty. How's it going?" Katherine asked.

"Awesome. You?"

She walked over to Marty and stopped a few feet away. She gave him the condescending look he dreaded seeing each visit. He almost missed it.

"I'm wondering what you and Steve were talking about."

Marty turned around, expecting to see Steve. He didn't see Steve.

Katherine laughed. It was creepy like when Tom Cruise laughed. "He snuck out through the kitchen. I had someone watching you."

"Those two women? Was it the busboy?"

"It was Bob from accounting. He was at lunch and saw you together. Guess who's getting his own office Monday morning?"

Marty sighed. He didn't even know who Bob was or what accounting department she meant. The paper barely had a staff anymore.

"Since you're still on my payroll I still own you. Which means talking to a non-employee about work related things is a big no-no." Katherine turned and waved at the two police officers. "These men are going to take you for a ride."

"Holy shit. You're having me killed?" Marty looked around to see if he could flee. Maybe he could hide in the alley. Maybe he'd find out where Steve went.

Katherine laughed again. Still creepy.

"No one is going to die. In fact, I want to have a real long conversation with you. From the beginning. Find out everything you know about your hires Cull and Jackson. According to the files, you interviewed and hired them."

Marty shook his head. "That was years ago. I had no idea they'd be such assholes. Pardon my French."

"You don't need to apologize. There are some big changes coming to *The Hidden Truth*, Marty. Lots of new faces around the office lately. A new breed of journalist." Katherine walked to Marty and put her arm around his shoulder.

He tried unsuccessfully not to flinch.

"Remember when we started? It was about the story. Getting to the truth. Searching for the answers to life's great mysteries. Not anymore. Now it's about squealing on your neighbor." Katherine smiled. "Who's wearing ladies' underwear around the house?"

Marty looked away.

"I'm sure Steve thinks he has a master plan to steal more money from me. As if the computer geeks didn't immediately see what he was up to. I let him choose the length of his rope to hang himself and see who else was involved." Katherine finally took her arm off of Marty. "I have to be honest...I would've bet it was you siphoning money from the company."

"No. It wasn't. I swear." Marty glanced at the two cops. He was going to jail. Prison.

Katherine waved her hand. "I know it wasn't only you. It was Cull. The funny thing is it was his own greed that got the spotlight shined on him...and you. If he'd left the money alone and Steve took some out of the account, you would've been arrested along with him. I guess you can thank Cull for being so greedy."

"I had nothing to do with it."

"Just stop with that. What were you and Steve talking about?"

Marty looked away. "He wants to have me get him inside the building, so he can do something with the app. I told him I wasn't interested."

She grabbed him by the chin and stared into his eyes. "Don't you lie to me or these nice police officers, who definitely have better things to do, *will* take you for a ride."

"I told him to meet me tonight across from the building. He'll be at the park. You can arrest him there," Marty said.

Katherine let go and turned to the police. "You boys have been a big help. I appreciate the assistance, but I can take it from here."

"I don't understand." Marty said.

She turned back to Marty. "Of course, you don't. You can't begin to fathom what's going on in this technologically advanced world we live in. How the *Hidden Truth* app has changed it all. For the better? There are those who would argue in the negative."

"What do you want me to do?"

"I thought it was obvious. I'm going to reinstate your badge privileges. You'll meet Steve tonight, right on schedule, and you're going to bring him inside the building and help him steal the technology he needs to shut down the app."

CHAPTER 18

Reincarnated Jim Morrison and Elderly Elvis Stole my Car and Phone!

Windows shattered above their heads as they ran hunched over, down the deserted hallway. Rocks cracked doors and paneling on the opposite side.

"We have to get out of here." Jackson put his back to a concrete column between banks of windows.

A wider hallway led into darkness. The other path continued around the perimeter along broken tile floors and chipped plaster.

"Well, looks like they've run out of bullets," Cull said around the corner in the darkened hallway. "Or they're saving them for when they catch up to us in here."

"Jesus, Cull, we got to get out of here. Or get away from the windows until they run out of rocks."

"We can't get away from the windows and get out of here both. We'll have to pick one. Door number dead or door number deceased."

Voices rose in the trees outside the broken glass down from where they stood. Jackson turned his head and listened. It sounded like the commotion retreated.

Jackson said, "Okay. We need a plan. Something better than keep running from the people trying to kill us."

"Running from people trying to kill us seems to beat the alternative of letting them catch us, don't you think?"

"There's so many of them now and we keep getting pushed farther and farther out. I don't even remember where the car is, if we could get back to it."

"It's crashed into a light pole a few blocks over. Boxed in by other cars. Back when they still had bullets. Don't think we're going back. We'll need to steal something else. Under the circumstances, I'm thinking a grand theft charge or even some time in jail is preferable to this." Cull's phone dinged and echoed through the halls. He drew it out of his pocket.

"You need to turn that shit off, dummy."

"You turned the notifications on. I need you to show me how to do it."

"Toss it to me before you get us found and killed."

Cull waved the phone at Jackson, but did not toss it. "Oh, I know where we are. Someone posted on *Hidden Truth* that we're trapped in the vacant library building southeast of Valdosta State."

"Georgia?" Jackson shook his head. "I didn't know we'd come that far. This can't be the same people chasing us since the track. Or since the Wal-Mart."

"They seem pretty determined." Cull scrolled. "Yeah, they've been sharing where we were seen for the last day or more. That couple at the hotel that tried to throttle you posted which way you were headed. They've had our license plate and a description of the car since then. We're going to need to keep changing cars and find a place to hide that ain't surrounded."

The phone chimed three more times.

"Goddamn it, Cull."

"They're posting about surrounding the exits before they sweep the building. This is a well-organized lynching here. We need to find a sewer tunnel or an air duct or something."

Glass fell from the window frame a few feet to Jackson's left. A shadow spilled over the floor at an angle. Cull pressed his back to the wall and lowered his phone to his side.

"They're down here. Both of them. This way."

Footsteps echoed from deeper around the perimeter wall. Jackson sprinted across from the column and they both charged into the darkness of the interior hall.

"This way. I see them. They're headed down here. Hurry."

They stopped at the base of a set of wide switchback stairs. Cull looked at Jackson, but Jackson shook his head. Footsteps crunched behind them. Someone fell and cursed. They cut to the left.

Cull's phone chimed again and sounded like a gong in the dark hallway. Jackson grabbed it out of his hand and silenced the notifications. Cull's passcode was still 1234.

"I'm almost dead…the phone's battery, I mean."

Jackson put it on low power mode and handed it back. Shadowed figures crossed the swatch of light at the end of the hall ahead of them as footsteps grew behind them.

They moved through broken double doors to their right. The ceilings vaulted above them and empty shelves lined a balcony floor up and to their right. A number of shelves lay fallen like dominos from the center of the room to crushed cubicle tables on the far left. In the paths between shelves around them, torn and wet books piled into hills of pulp and mold.

Glass shattered behind them and they ran forward, clamoring over one of the piles. Jackson slid down on his ass on the other side. Cull took a tumble and smacked face down on the concrete floor between shreds of rotten carpeting. His phone skidded to the base up an upright shelf. Cull snatched up his phone and they continued forward.

They hurtled another ridge of ruined books and prepared to take the next hill. Jackson hoped for a door on the other side.

A shelf popped a few stacks over. "They come in here or did they go around?"

"Had to come this way unless they flushed themselves down the toilet."

"Could have gone up the stairs."

"Well, that motherfucker with the buck teeth, and them other two went up the stairs, so we're looking in here."

"Smells like cat piss and death in here."

"Spread out. Yell if you see them."

Cull and Jackson crouched between mounds of pulp and stared between shelves up to where the stacks collapsed. They couldn't see their pursuers or how many of them were in here with them, but they heard them all around.

Something crashed and a cascade of other collapses followed on the other side of the cavernous room. The sound roared around them. They met eyes and then climbed the next hill.

"Motherfucker."

"Over there."

"You find them."

"The hell's going on?"

"Get me out from under this shit."

On the other side, they found a high wall. A set of stairs led to the balcony level. A smaller passage cut down underneath the stairs. Jackson led that way and Cull followed. The doors beneath the stairs were chained together, but one side had splintered off its hinges, leaving a narrow gap.

Jackson exhaled slowly and then slipped through into the inky blackness. Cull grunted as he followed. His shirt caught and the doors rattled as he forced his way through. Jackson felt his way along the curve of the stone walls until the passage cut sharply to the right.

He heard Cull breathing behind him. Cull's phone lit and he held it out as a shallow flashlight. Jackson regretted the low power setting.

Light reflected back off of puddles. More water dripped around them as they continued. Greater light rose from above and then they found themselves at the base of more stairs.

At the top, Cull raised his head slowly to look through the grimy glass. No one outside.

He fought the stubborn crash bar with a grinding pop. The door opened a foot and then halted on another chain. They slid through and let the door slam closed as they ran from the building.

Jackson crouched between bushes and spiny fronds. They could see a street ahead of them. Shops, foot traffic, parking meters.

Sirens sounded from a street on the other side of the building. Maybe near where they left the car.

"What do you see?" Cull said.

"Nothing. I'm just tired."

"Fuck. You want to take a nap?"

"Maybe wait on the police."

Cull cleared his throat and scanned the overgrown property behind them in the direction of the building. "Let's hope no one used the *Hidden Truth* app to out any of the cops' side chicks or bribery schemes. Huh?"

"Shit." Jackson bowed his head. "Do they really blame us for what the magazine is doing? We're not the only names on the website. Why aren't they going after Marty? That I could get behind."

"Maybe they are." Cull scrolled. "I don't see anything about him. Or the kid? Or Katherine? I think people we met to sell upgrades to started posting about us and it built."

"Shit. Shit." Jackson spit into the overgrown grass. "I wanted to try to get our names off the website, but we're way past that. If they know you were fucking with their money, Katherine won't do anything to help us either. The mob will do the work for her."

"Which mob?" Cull said. "The Mob with a capital 'M' or the lynch mob behind us with a lowercase 'm'?"

"Oh, shit. We have to get out of here and figure something out."

"Okay." Cull stood and walked down the slope. "I have a plan."

Jackson looked over his shoulder and then followed. "We need the app down. We need to crash it."

Cull shook his head as they emerged on the sidewalk and Jackson waited to hear bullets ring out. Cull said, "This thing is global. If it hasn't crashed, it's not going to."

"Why are we the only assholes being hunted down?"

"We're not. There've been a bunch of revenge killings in India. Some pedo in California got chased up and down the Interstate. As far as I can tell, the police just let the crowd have him. Another guy that let people die in an old folks' home in England is on the run, too."

"When did you see all that?"

"When you were driving."

"You didn't think to tell me that we were…."

Cull walked away. A young man with blond hair ran his phone over the top of the parking meter, turning it from red to green.

Cull grabbed the phone away from him. "Give me your keys."

"Fuck you. Give it back." The guy reached.

Cull tripped the man and shoved him to his back on the sidewalk. "Keys, Asshole."

Cull wrestled them out of the man's pocket as the dude covered his face with his arms.

"Jesus." Jackson looked around hoping he both did and didn't see any cops.

Cull climbed in the driver's seat of the Corolla and unlocked Jackson's door. "Get in. We got to go."

"Give me my phone, Dude," the guy called from the ground.

"Fuck you." Cull pulled away from the curb while Jackson was still closing his door.

"What's the plan?"

"Stealing this car," Cull said. "That's all the plan so far. That and driving away as fast as we can before our fans find us again. Plug in my phone, will you?"

Jackson hooked Culls phone to the charger and cord in the stolen car, as Cull threw the stolen phone in the backseat.

"That kid's going to call the cops or worse, report us on the app."

"That's why I took his phone."

"If we call Steve and offer to give him the money back, do you think he could shut down the app? Just crash it himself."

Cull laughed as he made a right at the light and pressed the gas. "We took his password and gave it to Katherine. Remember? Well, you did."

"I took his password. You stole money from powerful, dangerous people. Want to discuss that again?"

"You have a point. Go on about the app."

"Yeah, we blocked Steve out, but he figured out how to hack the money. Maybe he can still screw with the app, if we can talk him into it."

"But I don't have the money anymore. Lost it on some investments at the track."

"He doesn't have to know that. We can play that we got it back somehow and are willing to trade."

Cull shook his head as he followed the signs to the Interstate. "If we ask him to shut it down, he'll just add something in to make us easier to find. He wants us deader than Katherine does."

Jackson took out his own phone. "I'm calling him."

"You'll make it worse."

"It can't get worse."

The back window shattered and both men ducked. Cull floored it.

CHAPTER 19

Myrtle Beach Werewolves Living in the Country Now Due to Rent Hikes and Gentrification

Steve had the literal keys to the kingdom. He just had no idea what to do with them.

Katherine and Marty were in the hallway arguing quietly but animatedly. He could see they were having a difference of opinion on how to proceed.

Steve had been given the master password to the site. Nothing held back. He was firmly in control. He felt like that fiddler guy while Rome burned around him.

"Why would we shut it down now?" Katherine -yelled at Marty. "You know how much money we have coming in on an hourly basis?"

"More like a minute by minute basis," Steve said, even though they couldn't hear him, too busy in one another's face.

At that moment, the servers were running double-time. It was close to capacity.

They were pulling in about $10,000 per minute.

$600,000 an hour. For the past six hours. All dumped into several accounts Steve now had access to. This moneymaker was making so much cash it was absurd.

All while the world went to shit around them.

"What changed your mind?" Katherine yelled at Marty.

"Maybe nearly getting killed tonight by an angry fucking mob in the park. Maybe I have a conscience. People are turning on everyone. The death toll is nearing uncountable numbers. The news media is guessing. There are so many riots and shootings and domestic violence cases right now it should make your friggin' head spin." Marty punched the glass partition in the hallway. "We're ruining the world."

"*The Hidden Truth* isn't responsible. We share no liability. Everyone signs an electronic waiver before they can use the app. Our lawyers have shielded us nicely from lawsuits." Katherine was no longer screaming, but she'd opened the door to the office Steve was seated in. "We're going to keep this going as long as we can. Until we milk it dry. I need to see ballsy soldiers today, manning their posts, Martin. Then and only then." She walked over to Steve, who had one eye on the money and another on this ruthless bitch headed his way.

Steve switched screens back to the raw data coming into the servers.

"How are we looking, Steve?" Katherine asked.

"Like everyone but me is making money on this," Steve said. If she was looking for ballsy, she was going to get it. He'd seen enough to know this was all going to crash down sooner than later. There was too much money on the line as well as an app that had become weaponized. "I don't get it. I did all the heavy lifting. I put this all into motion with only a promise of the riches to come. I got nothing in return. You were so quick to toss me onto the street. Now, suddenly you're acting like you're my best friend. Like you want to fuck me in a conference room, you love me around so much. What gives, lady?"

Marty looked like he was going to throw up.

Katherine didn't flinch. Didn't blink. She just kept staring at Steve like he had just told her she looked nice in her pant suit.

"I didn't get into the position I'm in by having feelings and stupid shit cloud my judgement. You want to know why, a few days ago, I had you tossed on your bony ass and, today you're getting the luxury treatment? Because today I need you. I need you to make sure everything is secure. I need you to skim the money out of the bank accounts and put them somewhere safe. The group I'd hired to do your job yesterday tried to steal my money. *My* money. They thought we'd be shut down by the government by now. This would all go away." Katherine was still smiling. "Guess what? We will be shut down soon enough.

How quickly doesn't matter. What does matter is getting all the money out. Now. Can you do it, Steve? Can you help me?" She touched his face. "There are many, many conference rooms in this building."

Marty did throw up, into a small wastebasket in the corner.

"I could just steal it," Steve said. It wasn't like he hadn't already thought of it. Or done it before.

Katherine shrugged. "That would be your prerogative. Maybe I brought you back in because I know you're not a thief. You're going to be the voice of reason in all this. Steve, you can help me to end this thing...when the right time is upon us. I have all the faith in the world you'll do the right thing when it matters."

"Kid, I hope you're not buying her line of bullshit. She's going to use you like she's used the rest of us." Marty laughed, but it turned into another puking session.

"Don't listen to that sick bastard. I'm sure you've seen the twisted things he does in his own house. Martin is the kind of guy who has made us rich." Katherine leaned over Steve and he could see down her shirt. Her black bra was holding up her tits nicely. "He forgets his place and the gravity of his sins."

He had to look away. He knew what she was doing.

"You mean making you rich." Steve stared at the numbers in amazement as they increased. It was up to fifteen grand a minute.

A fucking minute. A bigger blow up than Bitcoin. Some people were paying with Bitcoin too, in fact.

"Take a million," Katherine said. She leaned forward, but it wasn't to give Steve another show. It was to look closer at the screen. "We have, what, twenty million in the accounts? I'll give you ten percent when this is ready to be closed down or take a million now. Your call."

"Don't sell your soul to this devil," Marty said, coughing up small chunks into his hand. "Shut it down now and hope we can escape the building in one piece."

Katherine shook her head. "We're holding position until the police arrive."

"If they arrive." Marty sat down in a chair and put his elbows on the conference table. "Have you looked outside lately? Cops ain't coming downtown. They'll let it all burn first."

"You've always been so negative. I'm amazed you've lasted this long in this business," Katherine said. Steve thought she was trying to hide a smirk when she said it to Marty. She was actually enjoying this chaos. She enjoyed having him by the balls and owing her his continued freedom. Maybe his life.

"I knew I should've never come back. I got kids, you know. My daughter lives near Myrtle Beach. Married a teacher. She said he's a nice guy, too. They got a couple of kids, I think. Maybe they were trying for kids. I don't remember." Marty stared at the ceiling. "I've wasted my life making up fake news when a real life was always in my reach."

"Fake news…" Katherine slapped the table. "Don't be so dramatic, Marty. Your life has been a sham since we met. I knew you'd be the perfect editor for the lies we printed. You know why? You don't have a backbone. You're weak. You think no one knows what a sick little man you are with your twisted ideas and your deviant behavior." She looked at Steve and winked. "Martin doesn't think I know what he does late at night when he thinks no one is around. He logs into the app and reads disgusting and illegal sexual perversions and jerks off into a pair of women's underwear in his top drawer."

Marty jumped up like he was going to challenge Katherine, but she put up a finger and he dropped back into his chair.

"And then he thinks he can steal from me. What about you, Steve? You got any crazy hang-ups like Marty? Anything our platinum members would pay dearly to read? You into Asian boys? Like to shove gerbils in your butt? Huh? What is it?"

"I like to cuddle after sex," Steve said and stared at the screen. "And then steal from the guys stealing from you, I guess." What was he going to do to get out of this? The streets would be a mess right now.

Only one way to find out.

He logged into the security system. He no longer cared what Katherine knew he could or couldn't do. He needed to see what was happening.

The mob surged outside. Down on the street. Even with the

wide angle of the cameras he couldn't see the end to the crowd. Most were standing around, waiting for the fuse to be lit before they exploded.

Steve knew they were screwed.

"Shut down the app," Marty said. He was crying now, tears running down his fat cheeks. "It's the only way we get out of this alive."

"If we shut it down, we'll have no leverage. Holding onto it is the only move we have left," Katherine said. "Can you back it up so we don't lose anything?"

Steve shrugged. "It will take a few hours to do, but I can do it." He was lying. He could copy everything they needed from the code onto an external drive in a few minutes. The site was already backed up on other servers unless he cleared those himself. He'd need to also back it all up to a secured server of his own, so there would never be a problem getting back to it. Just in case he needed his own leverage. "I just need you to leave me alone, so I can work. Find me a sandwich or something to drink."

"I have bourbon in my office," Katherine said.

"I was thinking more soda, but alcohol will work in a pinch." Steve pointed at Marty. "You need to do something with him. He's quite distracting. He smells and he's loud."

"I'll put him in an office with a couch. Hopefully, he'll sleep it off. Anything else?" Katherine grinned.

"Yes. I want five million dollars. No matter what. Agreed?"

"Can you make it happen and slide the rest into my account?"

"Of course. It will add an hour to my time," Steve lied.

"Then, do it."

Steve nodded. "I'll need the bourbon and Marty gone so I can concentrate. Don't leave the building."

Katherine stared at the camera angle on the screen. "I don't think I could get too far. While my picture isn't anywhere on the app, I'd hate to have some asshole who's used Google figure out who I was."

The Hidden Truth is the only search engine anyone needs anymore, he thought. Steve wiped his face. "We're wasting time."

"I'll be right back." Katherine snapped at Marty. "Get up.

You've been promoted to CEO. You get the office, too. Feel free to relax on the couch. Move. Now."

Marty stood, wiping the slobber off his face. He stared at Steve. "What's happening?"

"I'm going to fix this. Make it all better, Marty. *If* you leave me alone for a few hours." Steve was getting antsy to begin, but they were taking too long. He glanced at the screen again. "They're trying to break into the building."

"It will hold for a while," Katherine said, but she didn't sound like she was too sure. This was the fancy office. The old mag office at the beach had burned to the ground. The riot probably doubled the population there. Then, the hivemind had located this office. Even this place wasn't designed to hold off an apocalypse though. "Just hurry up."

"Then, get out already," Steve said and gave her his best annoyed look.

Katherine narrowed her eyes. "I'm going to say this once… don't even think about screwing me over. Got it? Within the hour, I'd better get confirmation the money is in my account."

"Less five million."

She sighed and nodded. "Fair enough. I want the app secured, too. Even if I decide later to take it down or pause it, I need to make sure I can get back to it without a problem."

"Fair enough," Steve said. "Don't bother bringing a glass with the bourbon. I really do need something to eat, too."

"I'll tip over the vending machine."

Steve had a thought. "Before you go…where did you send Cull and Jackson?"

"I didn't sent them anywhere. They were on the run when your shitty scheme blew up. First from us and then from the mobs. Somewhere in Georgia now. I think. Why?"

"I just want to make sure they're safe, too. They might come in handy later on," Steve said.

Katherine smiled again, but it was more forced.

Steve nodded and watched Katherine walk out, hooking Marty by the arm as she moved past him. In the hallway, she looked back and looked like she wanted to say something more, but instead shook her head and left.

She was afraid Steve would take advantage.

Which was exactly what he was going to do.

He deposited the five million in his own account and skimmed the rest into Katherine's, but set it up so in twenty-four hours it would pull to an offshore account. No way to get to it.

Every penny made after two hours from now would feed into that account as well.

Steve checked to see the app was down to about eight grand every ten minutes. It was starting to slow as the infrastructure collapsed around them. More people devolving into chaos meant fewer people reading the stories on the app. They'd be too busy killing one another. Maybe the power grid was going down some places, too. It was going to be a real-life Purge without the twelve-hour time limit.

Once he'd made copies of all the pertinent files to a thumb drive, which he'd give to Katherine, but with the wrong password, and made sure he had it stored online in a couple of places only he could access, he went to work on the rest of his plan.

But first...Katherine was back with two glasses and a bottle.

Steve stood, blocking the computer screen. He rudely grabbed the bourbon and took a glass, throwing it against the wall.

Katherine didn't flinch.

"There's no time for games. I need to concentrate. These animals will be inside soon. We might not make it out alive. I want to make sure nothing happens. Right now, if they get to this floor, they could shut it all down." Steve reached for the other glass, but Katherine pulled it away.

"Don't fuck me." She slammed the glass against the wall and turned away.

Once Steve was sure she wasn't coming back he took a swig of bourbon before getting back to work.

He posted a picture of Katherine on the app website and sent it to everyone in the *Hidden Truth* contact list, which included most media outlets. She would now be the face of the problem.

Steve searched and found Cull's phone signal, placing him in a general area. They were close to Atlanta. Stupid move for men afraid of being mobbed to death.

He posted on the app itself where the two men were and how they'd been behind all of this mess in the first place, along with Katherine.

The people needed to have a face for the enemy.

Cull posted a plea on the app at that moment, begging people to let he and Jackson live. They'd do what they could to get the site shutdown and everyone's lives restored. The idiot left his locator on and people knew what highway they were traveling. Threats blew up like popcorn. It was too late. They had ruined everything. They were going to pay.

That was all true. Cull's stupidity and Steve's helping hand was going to turn Atlanta into a Purge for those two, back-stabbing bastards.

Steve did a search of the cameras in the building and mapped a quick escape route in his mind before setting the security doors to all open in thirty minutes, exposing it to a flood of animals bent on destroying everything in their path.

He just needed to get out as soon as possible without Katherine knowing it.

She'd think he bailed, but when she saw the money in her account, she'd believe he hadn't screwed her. Steve wished he could see her face when the money transferred out and was gone.

Satisfied he'd done everything he could to cover his own tracks, setup Katherine, Cull and Jackson, and make himself quite rich, Steve set the app to shut down in thirty minutes except for the pictures of public enemies number one, two, and three.

CHAPTER 20

Apple Slows Down Old iPhones to Steal Your Life Savings

The Toyota veered into the concrete median of I-75 North again. Sparks erupted off the side and the fender tore away this time. The bump bent into the wheel and twisted the works as the car bounced off the abutment under the overpass. The sudden shift to the right knocked down two men and a woman standing in the lane. But the car lost all its momentum from the impact with the concrete edge.

The three victims did not get up, but the dozens of others closed in from all around. As glass from both sides of the car shattered in on the two men inside, people cheered from the railings of the overpass above. The roar undulated in the darkness underneath.

They pulled the skinny one, in the back, out of the passenger's side window.

The fatter one behind the wheel crawled away as they tried and failed to open the driver's side door. One woman got hold of his hair and tore out a tuft along with a swatch of bloody skin.

The passenger kicked free and crawled along the road past the back tire. Before he could stand, they kicked him in his ribs and head. He tried to get a leg under him, but three people pushed him down to his face and belly again. He resumed his crawl through the kicks of his attackers, but did not make much more progress.

A few cars slowed, but then sped on past the scene.

The angry crowd found rocks and rained them down on his

head. They picked the bloody pieces up to stone him over again with the same chunks of concrete.

People joined in with boards, tire irons, and other metal discarded along the road. He didn't crawl anymore, but it took him a long time to die. They kept hitting him after that, too.

People recorded with their phones. One man, barefoot and only wearing jeans, circled out into the lanes to get a better angle on the man's bloody head on the ground. "How you doing, fam? How you doing, fam? We gotchu. We gotchu, didn't we, fam?"

A Ford tried to swerve at the last second, but the barefoot man tumbled ass-over-head across the hood, the roof, and off the back of the car's high trunk. He bounced twice in the highway behind the car, but never let go of his phone even after he was out cold. The Ford sped away with a cracked windshield.

The driver of the Toyota held onto the seat and steering wheel as three people pulled at his legs. Another man hopped onto the hood and laughed as he filmed mostly his own reflection in the windshield. "The truth ain't so hidden anymore, is it, Motherfuckers?"

A woman used a skinny steak knife to stab at the back of the driver's thighs. She accidentally caught the hand of a man pulling on the driver. The man cursed in a language she did not understand and then punched her in the face.

The other two dragged the driver out and everyone swarmed. The man on the hood tried to get an overhead view, but there were too many bodies and too much blood. They tore out the dude's eyes and ripped off his lips. The man with the stabbed hand caved in the driver's teeth and came away with two teeth embedded in the knuckles of his good hand.

The driver died quicker than the passenger and there wasn't much left when everyone stepped back to snap pictures for the app's message boards.

The whole time, Cull's phone continued to send out a signal from under the driver's seat.

In a Dodge, moving southbound, Cull scrolled through Jackson's phone from the passenger's seat. "I lost the screen. Your phone is set up all different from mine. How do I get back to it?"

"Hold it up where I can see it." Jackson looked back and forth from the road. "Your screen must look different because you don't update your apps. When was the last time you ran an update?"

"I hate that shit. Moves everything around and everything looks different."

Jackson tapped the screen twice and then put both hands back on the wheel. "There. What is it saying?"

"Oh, shit. That's gruesome. You want to see?"

"Just tell me what people are posting."

"It's moving fast. Lots of comments." Cull scrolled back toward the top. "They ripped those two guys apart. Tons of video and pictures. Oh, shit, that hippie asshole just got launched by a car. Looks like a vegan ragdoll."

"Do they think it was us? They thought the last message came from your phone, right? Can anyone tell it's not us from the pictures? This is important."

Cull shook his head. "No, they're all dancing on our graves. I'm scrolling through the pictures. Lots of blurs and bloody messes. No one is going to be able to tell shit."

"Have they looked in the wallets yet?"

Cull scrolled. "I can't fucking tell. It's just a bunch of trolls wishing they were there to murder us and then fuck us and then murder us again. Our licenses are in their wallets, if anyone checks and my phone is under their seat. Poor bastards thought we were robbing them. I bet they wish that's all we were doing. Of course, they're probably not wishing much of anything anymore now that they've been slaughtered. Don't think we're going to get our wings and halos when we do die one day."

"At least we can get back down to the offices and try to fix some shit without anyone chasing us anymore."

Cull whistled. "Holy shit." He drew the word *holy* way out like he was singing it. "Those dudes look like they got ripped apart by chimps. You ever seen those videos where crazy ass chimpanzees lay into someone, clawing off faces and biting off dicks? That's what these two look like now. They barely have faces anymore."

"Good."

Cull glanced at Jackson and shook his head. He chuckled. "Damn. Cold as ice."

"No, I meant they won't get identified as anyone else and maybe we won't get found out. That's all I'm…. Why the hell am I explaining myself to you? You were right with me setting those guys up for this."

"Better their asses than mine." Cull lowered the phone. "Let's stop to eat."

"Are you crazy? We just died. We need to let everyone find out before we go showing our faces again. We need to get back down to where this whole thing can get shutdown."

"We're a few hours away. We'll need to eat. Come on."

"Let's get back into Florida at least," Jackson said.

"Then, speed up. I'm hungry."

"So we can get pulled over in a stolen car with licenses of dead men that don't look like us? No thanks."

"When's the last time you saw a cop?" Cull waved with the phone toward the windows around them. "The ones who are still alive are busy as hell, but they aren't pulling over speeders or running plates."

"So, what makes you think fast food is still open?"

Cull sighed. "Shit. I hope you're wrong about that. Really will be the end of the world, if I can't get a burger and fries anymore."

"We need to get this shutdown and then I don't know what. Hide?"

"We should break in somewhere and cook some burgers before they go bad. Power's out in half the towns we passed since dark." Cull held out Jackson's phone. "How do I get the screen back again?"

"Fucking useless. You might as well not even have a phone."

"I don't. It's in the car where I died."

Jackson looked back and forth. He scrolled and tapped, but couldn't get what he wanted. His eyes went wide and he swerved off the road. A horn blared behind them and then past them.

Their headlights lit the shoulder of the highway and Jackson grabbed the phone away from Cull.

Cull said, "What the hell's wrong with you?"

"Oh, shit. Oh, shit. Oh, shit."

"What?"

Jackson showed his and Cull's pictures on the screen. He scrolled up to Katherine Hemingway and Marty and then back down to them. "It *has* been shut down. There's nothing left on the site except for our pictures and a single message claiming this was all our fault. Our little buddy Steve has fucked us but good now."

Cull took the phone back. "The site's down though. No one can track us even if they thought we were still alive. Right? Everyone who still has a cell signal is blind now. Unless they start a 'Murder Cull and Jackson' page on Facebook. Even then, only a fraction of the people who like the page will actually see the posts. We're good, right?"

Jackson drummed his fingers on the steering wheel. Several miles ahead and off to the left of the highway something exploded. A mushroom of flame belched up into the sky before breaking apart into darkness again. Three cars whizzed past them southbound one after the other.

"Jackson?"

"I don't know. If they have nowhere else to look, they may all start hunting us."

"They think we're dead though." Cull shook his head. "It worked. They thought it was us."

"I don't know how many saw it before the site went down. Now all there is to see is this." Jackson pulled back onto the highway and picked up speed toward Florida again. "We aren't stopping for burgers though."

CHAPTER 21

John Belushi Talks to Me from the Grave!

Sergeant Gino Smythe had served two tours in Operation Desert Storm. Killing the towel-heads on a daily basis and getting back to the base in time for chow and a poker game.

He'd once killed thirty-six people in a towel-head village because it was in his way. He could've gone around it, but why go through the trouble? He hated these inferior people anyway.

His men had followed orders without question. Most of them were as racist as he was. He'd put feelers out on base during his poker games or while watching a movie in the common area.

Surrounded himself with like-minded individuals.

Like he'd done when his service to this great country and Uncle Sam was over. He'd joined the police force and sworn to protect.

Well, the ones he wanted to protect, anyway.

He'd traded in his hatred of towel-heads for the fucking Spanglish-speaking motherfuckers who crowded the city. He especially hated the inferiors who couldn't speak a lick of English, yet they took jobs from real Americans.

Sergeant Smythe relaxed in his police cruiser two blocks from the action. He had no desire to fight English-speaking citizens who were just pissed about a phone app. Let them tear one another apart. He'd pulled his team back from the fighting. He knew he'd be in deep shit if the Police Chief got wind of it.

Fuck that guy. He spoke English, but he wasn't a real American. The guy was a few generations from being a slave.

Shoulda never let them boys free, if you asked Gino.

He was working his ass off, so they could get on welfare and have a dozen kids and work the system. *Fuckers....*

Sergeant Smythe's train of thought was broken when he saw the guy walking down the street, wearing a black hoodie. He kept looking back behind him. He was coming from the riot.

Gino stepped out of his vehicle and gave a nod to his team, who were jammed into two police vans parked behind him.

He knew they were itching to go kick some ass, but he didn't want to lose anyone. Not yet. There were a couple he didn't trust. He'd send them down the street first. If the Cuban and the Puerto Rican didn't get killed right away, the three blacks would go next.

No use in getting a good white man killed when it didn't need to happen.

"Hey...where ya headed, buddy?" Smythe had his hand on his holster as he moved across the street to intercept the man.

Instead of stopping or responding, the guy in the hoodie kept walking, now trying to veer to his left and get to the next intersection.

Smythe heard doors open behind him. His men, antsy and wanting to face an opponent, were going to get involved.

"Get back in the van," Smythe shouted over his shoulder. "I got this punk."

He didn't know if the guy was white or an inferior, but he'd find out.

Smythe took out his weapon and ran at the guy, who finally stopped when he saw his escape route had been cut off.

"Don't make a move. Take your hands out of the hoodie. Slowly. Let me see your face," Smythe said. If the guy made any sudden move, he'd shoot him. Just say he was reaching. They were always reaching, when you needed them to be. "Where ya comin' from?"

"Uh...down the block. Trying to get away from the fighting." The guy slowly moved his hands up and pulled down the hoodie.

Smythe relaxed. "White guy. Good. What's going on over there?"

The guy was staring past Gino as he spoke. "Fighting. People are insane. The cops are being pushed back. Lots of blood in the streets."

Smythe smiled. "You lose your appetite for it?"

"I have nothing to do with this. I just want to go home."

"Where's home, kid?"

The guy shuffled his feet. "Biloxi in Mississippi."

Smythe nodded. "You're a long way from home. How'd you get over to Florida?"

"It's a really long story. Can I go?"

Smythe waved him past. This guy wasn't trouble. Just a real American trying to survive.

As the guy increased his pace and headed down the street, Smythe turned to see the inferiors from his team standing in the middle of the street.

The rest of his team, the white guys he trusted, were hanging just outside one of the vans.

"Everyone back to your positions." Smythe took two steps and realized no one was moving. No one had obeyed his direct order. He stared at one of the blacks, an obnoxious guy who thought he was important to his team. "Didn't you hear me, boy?"

"I heard you loud and clear." The guy glanced at the rest of the men. "I also heard some of the things you've been saying on that racist podcast and shit. You think we wouldn't find out?"

Smythe sighed. He didn't have time for this shit. "Get back in the van. Last warning. I'm giving you this one pass, boy."

"Stop calling me 'boy,' you damn redneck racist motherfucker." The guy had his weapon in hand and aimed it at Smythe's face.

"Have you lost your fucking mind, officer? Stand down." Smythe glanced at the important part of his team, the white guys, but they were watching at a distance. Did they not see what was happening?

Smythe didn't know if he could get his weapon pulled and shoot before he was gunned down. While he knew these inferiors weren't as fast as he was or any white guy, the others had now drawn their weapons. He'd never be able to take them all out.

"I could use a little help over here," Smythe yelled to his real team. The guys that mattered.

The one aiming at his head smiled. "You think just because you share a shade of skin with them, they're on your side? They follow the shitty doctrine you follow? Hell no. They're *our* brothers. Not yours. They know right from wrong. They got our backs. Their color is blue."

Smythe couldn't believe what he was hearing, but his eyes weren't deceiving him. The fuckers were turning their backs on him. *Him.* A damn proud white man.

He put his hand up and took a step back. "Listen...you're all going to be fired for this. No pension. No unemployment. Your kids will be fatherless." He wanted to add how they probably didn't even know who their damn kids were, but he knew the situation was not in his favor. He'd kept his racist remarks in check all these years. No one had known his views. He was a professional. "I can diffuse this. Put down your weapons and we'll head back in. The stress has gotten to all of us. We'll work it out."

The white guys got into the van without looking back.

"Actually, you're no longer in command. This is how it's gonna work. Get on your knees. And don't reach."

Smythe wanted to argue, but now they were surrounding him.

He got down on his knees, begging them to reconsider.

One of the men pulled Smythe's weapon from his holster.

"Your Klan bullshit was all over the app. We've been keeping it in for a couple of days," the new leader said. He put the gun to Smythe's forehead. "The rest of the team helped with this plan. We knew what a chickenshit you were. You weren't going to get in the middle of a riot. Your normal method is to hang around the fringe of something big and wait until it's almost won by another team before we get to swoop in and take the credit. Frankly, we were all getting sick of you being a such a coward even before we had solid proof of your racist bullshit."

"Don't do this, you inferior piece of shit," Smythe said. "You don't have the balls." He pushed his head against the weapon. They were bluffing. No way they'd kill him on the street like a dog, especially when good men were in the van. He'd be the chickenshit. His real team would step out and tell him to stop and—Sergeant Gino Smythe felt a second of pressure before the bullet tore the thought out of the front-center of his brain.

At the sound of the gunshot from the block he'd just been harassed on by the cop behind him, Steve began to run.

There weren't people on the street in front of him, but he could hear the angry mob on the next block over.

I just need to get as far away from downtown as possible, Steve thought. *Hitch a ride back to Biloxi.* As if it would be simple. It wasn't just downtown that was under siege. It was the damn world. All because of the app.

A police car drove through the intersection ahead and Steve reflexively flattened against the wall. He didn't need to be stopped again, if he could help it.

Something exploded in the distance, a low muffled blast that Steve could feel as he began walking again. The city was coming apart around him.

Is this what the apocalypse was supposed to be? The world wasn't going to end with zombies or nuclear strikes. It was going to end because the *Hidden Truth* app had shared the most secret of secrets.

Steve had walked at least six blocks and as the noise at his back grew fainter, he began to relax. He knew he wasn't walking all the way home, but with each step further away from the office building and Katherine, he felt better.

Turning a corner, he saw a cafe which looked open. As he approached, he saw there were a few customers inside, eyes glued to their laptops and phones.

The place looked like it was serving coffee, as if the city wasn't falling down around them. Someone had spray painted the corner of the building with FITZEE WUZ HERE, but everything else looked like business as usual.

Steve knew he needed a car to get out of town. At this point he wasn't averse to stealing one if he had to. Maybe he could sweet talk someone into giving him a ride and then carjack the vehicle.

Is this really who you've become? Thinking about who to carjack like it's nothing? Holy shit, dude, you're a fucking mess. Steve tried unsuccessfully to shut his inner voice up.

His inner voice was right.

Steve entered the cafe and no one bothered to look up from their technology. Not even the bored-looking blonde behind the counter, who was tapping her phone like mad.

"Can I get a latte?"

The girl glanced at Steve and frowned. "Damn app is down."

Steve smiled. "Make it a large, please."

She shrugged, threw her phone on the counter, and went to hopefully make his drink.

Steve turned to survey the customers and see who he could get a ride from.

It didn't look promising.

Everyone looked too cool to talk to him. Every guy in the place except for Steve had a man-bun. The women ran the gamut from purposely dressing like they were homeless with no makeup and unkempt hair, despite the expensive laptop they were using to like cat pictures on Facebook, to a striking redhead in the corner wearing bright red lipstick that matched her red blouse and her high heels. She didn't have her head buried in an online search for funny memes.

She was staring at Steve with a Mona Lisa grin on her lips.

He did what any sensible dude would do when confronted with an alarmingly attractive woman noticing him: he turned back to see where his damn coffee was.

The girl at the counter didn't say another word as she took his last couple of dollars and handed over the coffee.

Steve turned back to the common area of the cafe.

The woman in red was still staring.

Every fiber of his being told him to run out the door and keep running until he saw the sign for Biloxi.

Instead, he smiled and walked boldly to the woman's table. "Is anyone sitting here?"

She grinned and pushed out the chair across from her with her red heel. "Great seat to watch the end of the world from. I've been coming back here each day to witness what terrible things we are all capable of."

CHAPTER 22

Trump Replaced by John Candy's Body Double in 1999

Marty's eyes went wide as he screamed into the gag in his mouth. The pressure in his head built until he thought his eyes would pop out. Part of him hoped they did because he didn't want to see what was happening anymore.

The tie tasted like ass. It was wretched and salty on his tongue. It didn't help that it was his tie. The wad of felt in his mouth, behind the tie, was worse. It was used for cleaning computer screens and still had antiseptic taste of the spray people put on it. He told the bitches in the Flagler office to stop using the spray. Katherine's Jacksonville office and the people who worked there – used to work there – didn't know it was meant to be used dry, either. Wadded in his mouth it induced a thick, sticky saliva which stuck in the back of his throat like glue. The cloth absorbed liquid and then forced him to produce more.

He tried to work the back of his tongue to push the felt to the front of his mouth, but he kept drawing it back deeper. He sensed claustrophobic suffocation coming on. He kind of wished he was dead right then, but choking out on a computer screen cleaning cloth was too much.

Then, there was the dude squeezing both of Marty's nipples and twisting in opposite directions.

"Two of those fuckers are dead. Tell us where the bitch is."

The dude with the shaved head behind the fat, bearded Charles Manson with the nipple fetish said, "He can't say anything with the gag in his mouth."

"He has to know we're serious or he won't stop saying 'I

don't know' every time we ask." Fat Manson let off Marty's raw nipples, but kept rubbing them with his thumbs. Somehow much worse.

Marty twisted his hands back and forth where they were tied behind the back of the wooden chair with an extension cord. His ankles were bound by packing tape.

Glass shattered out somewhere on the main floor and furniture smashed in multiple rooms.

"If she's in the building someone will find her. We're wasting our time in here. There could be good shit in here. Like a safe with money in this guy's office or hers, right? Ask him where that is."

I don't have an office or a safe. My office burned down in Flagler.

"Okay, give me something sharp."

Shaved Head looked around. "You going to cut him loose?"

"No, I'm going to cut him up and make him tell us where the money is."

The felt lodged in Marty's throat. He was surprisingly unpanicked for the first couple seconds. He was focused on the sharp object talk and then, he was just trying to get the cloth moved with his tongue. After that, he convulsed and his eyes rolled up in his head.

"He's faking," Fat Manson said.

"His mouth is frothing. You shoved it in too far."

Shaved Head pulled the tie out of Marty's mouth and tossed it to the side when the knot slipped out. He tried to reach between his teeth. Marty wasn't aware of what was going on. He could hear voices, but his vision had gone dark. His body shook hard enough in the chair that the tape ripped away from his ankles and his legs quivered out straight.

"I can't get it. It's too far down and he keeps trying to bite me."

Fat Manson stuffed his thick fingers into Marty's mouth and got hold of the cloth. All Marty registered was the taste of onions. Manson jerked the wet felt out in one motion and slapped it soggy onto a folding table.

Marty gagged and wretched and his vision came back. He bent over and drooled into his lap and heaved, but nothing left his stomach. He pictured his belly full of felt and packed into place.

He raised his eyes on the two men over him and the world seemed oddly unreal from his oxygen starved brain.

"This is fucked up," Shaved Head said. Marty thought the man was talking about the felt stuffing in his stomach and Marty was embarrassed they knew about it.

"We should take out our dicks now that his mouth is good and greasy."

"What the fuck did you just say?"

"I'm just joking."

Someone ran by the door. "We found her. She's running down the stairs. Take him back to the room with the others."

Shaved Head ran out the door. "Take him to the storage room with the others. I want to see when they get her."

Fat Manson faced the door and waved like he was saying goodbye to someone on a slowly receding ship to Europe. "I'll keep an eye on him until you get back."

Marty rubbed his fingers together because they felt weird and numb. He couldn't tell if they were cold or wet. Sometimes he had that trouble with clothes in the dryer, too. As he pressed his fingers together, the extension cord fell away from his wrists. He brought his hands around in front of him like he was surprised to see them.

Fat Manson still faced the door as he unzipped.

A shot glass worth of adrenaline pumped through the fading haze of oxygen deprivation and told Marty he had to get the hell out of this room or he was going to have worse than cleaning felt in his mouth and belly.

His muscles tightened and his stomach ached. He thought he was about to lose bowel control. Marty stood on wavering legs and grabbed up the chair behind him in an awkward twist of his torso.

Fat Manson turned with both hands on his junk. Marty let out a choked squeal and twisted in place. One of his feet slipped and he planted it again behind him as the chair made a hard arc through the air. To Marty, it felt like the chair moved under its own power and pulled him along with it.

He caught Manson with the thick front edge of the seat vertically over his face and watched the nose crush and the teeth come loose in his mouth. Marty expected the chair to break apart and the man's head to come clean off. Neither happened.

Fat Manson still held his dick as he tumbled backward over the folding table and stayed down. The wet felt stayed stuck to the table top even on its side like that.

The chair did pull Marty along in the follow-through. He dropped it and stumbled over his own feet toward the door. He got twisted up and slammed his back into the wall before sliding down to his ass.

Three people ran into the room. One of the guys held a butcher knife and pointed it at Marty on the floor. It was a fancy culinary knife. Made from one piece of solid steel from handle to point with a thick grip and sleek lines all the way through. Marty was embarrassed he knew the exact price because he had looked up that exact brand back when he was planning for a life where he had it made.

He stole from Katherine. Steve, Cull, and Jackson stole from him. Katherine stole back. Then, Steve murdered them all.

"What the hell happened in here?"

Marty pointed into the hallway. "The one in here beat our asses with a chair. You had to see him run out. He said there's a shit ton of money in his office. We need to get his ass."

They ran back out the door.

Marty stood and looked down at the heap of Fat Manson. He wished he had something sharp in here, too.

He stepped out into the hall and walked into the main room. People still smashed furniture while others ran down the stairs.

Marty grabbed up a plant off a shelf and threw it against the wall. The pot didn't break, but dirt went everywhere. He picked up papers and ripped them. He threw the pieces in the air. He grabbed a ceramic coffee mug off the floor and threw it down again. It bounced, but still didn't break. He had to figure out who made that. Marty kicked a trashcan which was already turned over.

Someone at the window shouted, "She's on the street. They got her."

Everyone ran to windows including Marty. He followed the flow of the crowd with his eyes and then caught sight of the figure wearing a business suit dress and running shoes ahead of them.

Sensible shoes? What the hell is this?

"That's a dude," Marty said.

The man in the dress pulled ahead of the crowd toward the next intersection, but they still chased.

Two vehicles roared across and screamed to a stop. Men with AR-15's stepped out of every door. The crowd still ran.

"This is going to be ugly."

One of the armed men tossed a rifle to the dude in the dress and he caught it. He turned and some in the crowd faltered. The men opened up and dropped the ones in front. Everyone at the windows recoiled. A few dropped to the floor, but Marty remained standing. The survivors in the crowd on the street retreated, but more were gunned down. The men actually reloaded and continued to fire.

Another set of SUVs pulled away from a curb on a cross street. Marty leaned forward and followed their course to the right.

"I'll be damned. She got away."

People in the building started to scatter.

Marty turned around and saw Shaved Head standing by another window, but staring at Marty. He realized at that moment, under the gaze of Shaved Head, that his own shirt was ripped open.

His chest had handprints on it. Someone with thick fingers. Marty remembered the taste of onions, but didn't understand why. The skin around his nipples was bright red.

Marty looked away from the red marks and shrugged. "What the fuck are you looking at?"

Shaved Head smiled and shook his head.

Marty took the stairs.

CHAPTER 23

Why Global Warming Is A Myth—Blame the Aztecs!

She was gorgeous. Steve committed every curve of her body, the twinkle in her smile, and the plush set of lips to memory. He knew it was such a cliché, but she was his Lady in Red.

Tonight, if he survived and got somewhere private, he'd open his mind's spank bank and pleasure himself imagining her.

"You're staring at me so hard I can feel my ass burning," Anna said and laughed when Steve blushed and turned away. "Oh, shit. You're not used to a woman being upfront with you. How quaint."

"My mother taught me not to stare," Steve said.

"And yet you were staring at me from the second you walked in."

Steve shook his head. "Not true. I came in for coffee." He lifted the cup as if she couldn't see it on the table. "Nothing more."

"I'm Anna, but for some strange reason friends call me Red."

"Steve. Friends call me Steve for some strange reason."

She leaned forward and put her elbows on the table. "That is strange. What are you doing here? People don't come for the overpriced coffee. They come to be seen or to hide. You don't have a laptop and you're not on a phone. You're out of place in the Post *Hidden Truth* World, Steve."

He decided he didn't have time to waste. "I'm looking for a ride."

"The Uber drivers hang out here?" She made a big show of looking around.

"I came in hoping to get lucky."

She grinned. "In what way?"

Steve started to blush and turn away, but forced himself to keep eye contact. She had gorgeous eyes, too. "Everything is crazy outside. I was hoping someone would give me a ride."

"How far?"

"As far as you'll take me?"

Red laughed. "Was that a question or an answer?"

"Both." Steve shrugged. He glanced around at the rest of the patrons, all acting like nothing was going on in the real world that could affect them. "I live in Biloxi."

"You're a long way from home, Steve."

"Tell me about it."

"Why are you in Jacksonville...and don't give me a bullshit answer." She leaned back in her chair and crossed her arms and legs. "I can tell when a guy is lying to me."

"I came here for a job. It didn't work out. Now I'm running out of money and need a ride home."

She stared at him. He was getting uncomfortable.

Steve stood up.

"Where are you going?"

He shrugged. "I'm running out of time. Downtown is like a warzone. I need to put some distance between me and a mob."

Now she was really smiling. "Holy shit. You have something to do with the *Hidden Truth* app. Are you a programmer? Fact-checker? Or did you come here for revenge against someone who posted about your Brony thing?"

"I don't have a Brony thing...I don't even know what that is."

Red squinted her eyes, but she was grinning. "I bet you'd look cute as a pink pony."

"What? Eww. Weird. No thanks," Steve said.

"The Brony doth protest too much, methinks."

Steve was having a hard time following this conversation. He had a bad feeling she'd grow bored with him quickly, since he was no match for her obvious intellect. *Relax, dude, you're not gonna marry her,* he thought. *You need to use her for a ride. That's it. Get your head out of your ass and take control of the situation for once.*

She pointed at her head. "Inner monologue going on inside, Brony Steve?"

"No. Yes."

She nodded solemnly, her smile gone, replaced with tight lips. He wanted to kiss her.

Steve sipped his coffee. He had no idea what she was going to say next. He thought he might be in love.

"You changed the subject about working for the app or not. You have something to do with it. Don't you?"

Steve shook his head.

"I can tell when someone is lying to me. You know why? Because I have what my grandmother used to call Seventh Sense. Ever heard of it?"

"No." Steve took another sip and looked around. Maybe someone else would give him a ride, or he could follow them to their car and take it.

"Good answer. Most dudes sitting in that seat will try to bullshit with me and say they've heard of it," she said.

"It's not real. You make shit up." Steve decided to go for it. Either she'd give him a ride, or he'd walk away and think about her tonight. "You hide behind the lines and the in your face attitude. Why? I think it's because, despite how over the top pretty you are, you have self-doubt. Someone in your past put you down. Led you to believe you were less than you were. Now you hide behind the wicked smile and batting your eyes to keep guys in the dark about the real you."

Actually, I thought I was more than I was. Thought I was the center of all of this. Turns out, the sordid past had nothing to do with me. The Senator was just tired of having me around, like always, and my family reminded me exactly how little of this was all about me, Steve. You need a ride and I need a new distraction. Let's play, shall we.

"You're in love with me," she said.

"Shut up." Steve remembered he was still standing at her table, which might've looked odd to anyone else, if they were actually doing something other than staring at their phones and laptop screens.

"I knew it. I've never been in love before. Not in the way people are supposed to be in love. It has nothing to do with a chemical reaction or using KY or love in the Biblical sense." Red stood. "Are you a virgin, Brony Steve?"

"No. I had a girlfriend."

"That doesn't automatically mean you had sex. Holding a girl's hand in third grade doesn't lose virginity."

"I've had plenty of sex," Steve lied. She was unsettling him again. He'd started out strong and was fading quickly. "Besides, you only need to do it once and you lose your virginity. It isn't like there's a certain percentage or how long you go before it's officially discarded."

"Can you go long?" Red asked, the grin returning.

"Can you give me a ride?"

Red sighed. "I'm not sure I should. My mama always frowned on hitchhikers. She's seen so many horror movies. Most of them are about picking up a stranger on the side of the foggy road in the middle of the night."

"It's only now sundown. There's no fog. You know me now."

Red pointed at him. "Brony Steve."

"Please, stop calling me that."

She shook her head. "Once you gain a nickname organically, it stays with you. If you want a ride from me, you'll have to let me call you Brony Steve. Even in front of other people. Especially anyone related to you, so I can hear you talk your way out of the nickname."

Steve felt the panic rising in him. The angry mob could begin moving street to street. Pulling people out of cafes and buildings. Looking for their pound of flesh.

He didn't want an ounce of his flesh to be pounded.

"Thanks for the lively conversation, but I need to get out of town. You have an awesome life, Red." Steve walked with his coffee to the exit, guzzling it down once he got to the garbage can near the door.

He looked outside, expecting to see torch-wielding villagers bent on destruction, but it looked like any other city street. Steve wondered how long it would last.

Once he'd finished his coffee, he tossed it in the garbage, under the FITZEE graffiti. He'd need to get a ride, even if it was just a few miles away. Some distance would clear his head. Help him think. He'd need to find a computer, too. Start to move some money around so he had walking around cash. A few hundred. Nothing ridiculous.

"No promises how far I'll take you." Red was right beside him. "I'd like an adventure. Plus, my schedule is unexpectedly clear right now. Let's go see where the road takes us."

He opened his mouth to speak, but Red put a finger to his lips and shook her head.

"I'm in the parking lot across the street. I hope you're not one of those jerks who hates a chick in a muscle car," Red said.

Steve heard the speeding vehicle before he saw it, bouncing down the street like it was out of control. He flattened against the wall of the cafe, afraid a wheel would spin off its axle and kill him like a cartoon.

"You gotta be shitting me," Steve said.

He'd glimpsed Katherine in the front seat and he'd locked eyes with her for a split second. She'd seen him, too.

Red was smiling at the chaos on the street as a convoy of cars, trucks and motorcycles sped by in pursuit.

She laughed and said, "Speak of the bitch."

Steve shook his head. He had two choices: he could convince Red to drive him back to Biloxi or at least get him out of Jacksonville or he could pursue Katherine, so she didn't escape.

Katherine on the loose meant, at any point, she could tell the world what his part in the app had been. Fuck. She could say anything she wanted to say, especially since she'd probably figured out Steve had fucked her over and saved his own ass. She could send anyone after him, better and more deadly than he could chase her down.

Like the fucking dog who catches the car and doesn't know what to do with it.

Steve took a deep breath and let it out.

"You said you have a muscle car? Do you drive fast or are you in love with your baby and don't want to chance it?" Steve asked.

"The only way to drive a Mustang is to drive fast, Silly." She pulled out her keys from between her breasts and grinned. "I think I'm in love with you, Brony Steve."

CHAPTER 24

Lizard People and Greys Schedule Peace Talks in Paris: The Fate of Earth Hangs in the Balance!

Cull shook as he dug his thumbs into the man's throat. He heard something snap and felt the cords and bones grind under his grip, but he wasn't sure he had crushed the works inside the asshole's gobbler or not.

His fingers ached, and his arms shook from fatigue. The dude's arms had finally fallen to the floor, away from scratching at Cull's eyes and clawing his face.

At one point, Cull thought the guy had gotten a good enough grip on his right ear to tear it clean off. The cartilage in that ear still throbbed and burned from the grip. He felt the redness and the heat across the entire side of his head. It happened to him any time he got boxed on one or both of his ears. Happened when his father or one of his brothers connected a shot there. They laughed at him about it growing up and sometimes tried to clip him on purpose just to see it even when he'd done nothing to provoke it – sometimes especially then. It happened when drunks in bars threw wild haymakers and caught an ear. Cull was shocked he wasn't cauliflowered on both sides by now.

Even with all that, this piece of shit's ear grab was worse than all the ear punches and flicks Cull could remember. This motherfucker, who offered to open late and let Cull and Jackson refuel and grab some drinks, had pulled a gun and then a knife on them because he knew who they were. Jackson and Cull had gotten him down on the floor of the dark gas station and disarmed. Cull had turned the gun on the dude and it clicked empty. Then, the asshole had kicked Cull in the nuts and punched Jackson in the kidney. Jackson lost his grip on the knife. It had slid between the wasabi flavored almond display and the motor oil. Dick Breath went for it. Cull got on the man's back and tried to lock in a rear naked choke like he'd seen on the TV cage fights. Turned out to be tougher to do than it looked on TV, and the piece of shit was on Cull for a ground and pound. Jackson clocked the guy with a rusty metal hubcap attached to the bathroom key. The guy went for the knife again and that's when the choking started.

Cull could just stab the dude, but it took so many stabs to actually kill someone even when they weren't fighting back. He knew that much over and over again from crime scene photography. He could beat the guy's skull in, but that still took a lot of hits to make sure he was dead. Not as easy to break a skull and kill a brain as the zombie movies made it look. If the gun had a bullet in it, Cull would gladly do that at this point, but the asshole tried to capture the two of them with an empty.

Strangling someone was a pain in the ass. It wasn't like Cull exercised at all much less the isometric exercise involved in squeezing a throat as long as it took to choke out life. Cull learned, from the cops he had paid off for photos over the years, that stranglers had to squeeze and release several times in order to kill someone that way. Even the ones in good shape.

Cull still felt a pulse under his hands, so he relaxed for a couple seconds and then squeezed back down to continue his inaugural strangulation. He tried to use his weight to add pressure to the squeeze. The guy wasn't fighting back anymore, so Cull didn't have to worry about being off balance and kicked off.

Jackson walked by from the back of the store toward the front doors. He drank from an orange juice and set a glass bottle down next to where Cull strangled the gas station attendant. Maybe this guy was the owner. Probably. Cull couldn't tell, and it didn't matter.

Sweat stood out on his forehead. Cull glanced at the bottle and then at Jackson's back. "What the hell is that?"

"It's that ice tea you like."

"Oh, the one with peach in it."

"They didn't have just the peach flavor. That is peach and mango."

Cull shook his head and sweat dripped into the closed eyes of the man on the floor under him. The guy's face twitched, but he didn't open his eyes and he didn't renew his fight.

"That's the second best one."

"Yeah, I know. You tell me every time we stop."

"You're sure there was no peach? Sometimes they mix the peach flavor with the peach and mango together because they don't pay attention. Sometimes it's behind the other ones."

"I looked, Cull. I always do. There were none. You can go look, if you don't believe me. There was peach in that other kind of tea with the green leaves on the bottle."

Cull relaxed his grip a few seconds and then bore down again. "That stuff is horse piss in a bottle."

"I know." Jackson took another sip from his orange juice as he scrolled through the gas station attendant's phone. "That's what you tell me, so I got you the second best of the tea that is not pissed out of a whore."

"You want to take over here, so I can get a sip?"

Jackson laughed. "Ugh, no, I do not want to tag team strangle that guy with you."

"Come on, man. He was trying to attack you, too. This is as much your problem as it is mine."

"I'm well aware, Cull, but I'm not doing it. I ain't going to miss the guy once he's dead, believe me, but I'll let you handle choking him to death. You're doing a fine job."

"You know, if this goes to court, you'll get convicted, too. They won't let you off because you stood there on the dead guy's phone drinking the dead guy's orange juice while I did it."

"I'm aware. Drinking orange juice while you strangle him is not my grand defense plan. I just don't want to do it. You can take a break to get a drink and then start back up again."

"Shit." Cull took a deep breath. "No. I don't want him catching his breath again and then this takes twice as long to finish. I'll just do it since you're going to be an asshole about it."

"You're a saint among men, Cull."

"Is this about the gambling thing with losing your car? Is that why you won't help me strangle this guy?"

"No, it has nothing to do with that," Jackson said. "If you hadn't done that, we wouldn't have met Steve and we wouldn't have gotten the app done and you wouldn't have been using him to steal from Katherine and whatever Mob her family is connected to and Steve wouldn't have locked it all down and sold us out and we wouldn't be here rich and famous and happy and safe like we are right this moment."

Cull rubbed his tongue through his dry mouth as he looked at the unopened bottle next to him. He tried to spit, but it came out thick and globbed with mucus, so it stuck to his chin. He started to ask Jackson to wipe it off for him, but then decided not to.

Cull said, "You could have just admitted you were pissed about all that and said that's why you won't help me."

"I'm not pissed at you," Jackson said. "Not anymore really. What difference does it make anyway? I hunted around for the peach tea and remembered your second choice. Do pissed people do that?"

"I guess not." The glob of mucus oozed down in a string off of Cull's chin and ran down the dude's cheek into his ear.

"Besides, we both have our individual talents in this partnership," Jackson said. "You do the pictures. I lead out on interviews. You embezzle money. I get us away from the people trying to kill us because you embezzled money. You're apparently talented with murder. I know how a phone works."

"See, now I think you're pissed again." Cull saw the string off his chin and wiped his face against his shoulder without letting up on the choke. "And most of the people trying to kill us are doing it for a bunch of reasons which have nothing to do with the money. Most likely, Steve put your and my pictures up with his final 'fuck you' move because of you cutting him out the first time."

"That's true. You did pull him back in though." Jackson lowered the phone and took another drink as he stared out at their vehicle by the pumps.

"Every time I try to get out..." Cull took a couple deep breaths and relaxed his grip. He was too winded to finish the movie line, so he let it go.

Jackson tossed the empty juice bottle onto the floor by the motor oil with a clatter.

Cull still felt a pulse. It was thready and weak, but still there. He gripped again and leaned his weight on.

"Did he make any calls?" Cull asked. "Is anyone coming, you think?"

"Not that I can tell." Jackson lifted the phone again. "It doesn't look like it. No calls for more than an hour before we got here. No text messages. I looked on Facebook messenger and didn't see anything. I don't think he posted at all about us. We should be good. I mean, I don't want to spend the night here, but we're in no more danger right now than out on the road."

"You think everyone knows now that we're not dead? This piece of shit recognized us."

"I don't know what people know. Some probably think we're dead. I don't know how many. There's cell service and power here, but not everywhere we drove through. Who knows who saw, who believes it, or who even remembers? At least there isn't an app for them to track us anymore."

"They'll recognize us from the pictures on the site now," Cull said.

"That's true. How close are you to being done with that turkey, Cull?"

"He's almost there. I just want to be sure."

"I'm going to delete all the apps on this guy's phone. It'll make it harder for anyone to track us and connect us to all this."

"You should bring it," Cull said. "It may be morning or later before anyone finds him. The way things were going could be days before it's properly investigated. We could dump the phone before then."

"Oh, shit," Jackson said.

"What is it? He did make a call? Tell me it wasn't 911."

"No, Marty just sent me an e-mail."

"You checked your e-mail on that phone?" Cull let go and fought to bend his fingers out straight again. "Yeah, you definitely need to delete everything on that phone and break the what's it called inside with all the stuff on it. You know what I mean?"

Jackson read the e-mail twice.

Cull stretched his back and then felt for a pulse. He climbed off the dead man and leaned against the cigarette ad on the base of the front counter as he opened his tea. He almost couldn't grip the cap enough to turn it. The safety top popped and he took a swallow. His hands kept trying to cramp up on him. Peach and mango wasn't bad, especially after all that exertion, but it wasn't nearly as good as just peach. Why screw up the best thing with something else added in?

"You want to meet up with Marty?" Jackson asked after his second read through.

"Are you joking?" Cull took another long swallow. "So he can hand us right over to Katherine and her professional murder squad? No, thanks. I was thinking maybe keep driving until we get to the Keys. Start new identities there. Or if that doesn't work, we build our own raft and float to Cuba reverse refuge style. I hear Havana is great this time of year. Compared to all this mess anyway."

"He says Katherine left him high and dry in her Jacksonville offices. People were trying to torture him and he fought his way loose from them."

Cull snorted and took another swallow. "That doesn't sound like Marty at all."

"He pretended to be part of the rioters and got out of the building."

Cull tilted up his half empty peach and mango. "Now that sounds like Marty."

"Steve screwed over Katherine and all of us. Did it while Katherine had him in the office to shut down the app."

Cull got down to backwash and set the glass bottle down next to him. "Now that sounds like Steve."

"Marty thinks he knows where Katherine is and he's following Steve. He thinks Steve took all the money from Katherine before he split. Thinks Steve got a ride from an accomplice and is racing back toward his old home in Mississippi."

Cull clicked his tongue. He realized he needed to piss, but he didn't feel like getting up yet. "Steve is getting his own accomplices now? I'm hurt. I feel so rejected."

"This was sent like minutes ago. They're passing right under us, if Marty is right."

"That's a great big 'if' if ever there was one."

"Marty wants our help to get Steve to take the pictures down and to get enough of the money to disappear. Doesn't care about everything else between us. He just wants to get away. What do you think?"

Cull shrugged. "Has to beat the zero plan we got now of just killing people for gas and tea."

"I'll message him back and see if we can catch up. Let's go."

Cull extended a hand from the floor. "Help me up. Some of us have been working here. I need to piss and we should grab up food and more tea before we go. I definitely need something harder to cut it with, too."

CHAPTER 25

Hitler's Remains Found Buried on Oak Island

Katherine ordered the driver to find a safe place, so she could use the bathroom, knowing as the world collapsed around them, it would be harder to find toilet paper and an intact mirror to use to re-apply her lipstick.

Confident with the well-armed men to guard her, Katherine felt invincible again.

She pushed the harrowing escape from the Jacksonville Annex out of her mind. There was never any use dwelling on the past. The only thing you could control was the present while manipulating things for a better future.

They got off the exit and pulled into a gas station. The other three SUV's curved out toward the road, but the men in those vehicles stayed inside.

"I'm going to need to get gas," her driver said.

"Then, do it. I need to use the little girl's room. One of you can accompany me." Katherine waited to see which one of them would smirk about it. See if either of them joked about going into the bathroom with her. Anything.

Nothing. Katherine sighed and slapped the one seated next to her in the backseat. "Go inside and make sure there's nothing wrong going on."

"Yes, ma'am." As he got out, machine gun in hand, the one in the passenger seat exited the vehicle and covered him.

This was the best grand a day Katherine had ever spent. Even better than the two strong cabana boys in Nicaragua in the late eighties.

She knew Steve had fled with the bulk of the money. Millions, in fact. Katherine wasn't mad. In fact, she was proud of the little weasel. He'd finally grown a pair of balls and done something for himself.

Katherine wasn't stupid and hadn't risen to his level because she'd never been careless or without several contingency plans in place at all times.

When she was sure Steve had taken the money and she'd gotten out of the building, she'd tapped into one of her many personal accounts in her real name.

Her daddy had been a mean sonofabitch before he'd gone to prison, but he'd taught his daughter quite a few things she was still using in life.

Childhood hadn't been dramatically horrible. She was never molested. Never beaten. Never forced to live in a broom closet and eat dog food.

Katherine had been trained to be better than everyone around her, and understand you only had one chance in life. Take it. Seize it by the balls. Never, ever worry about the next guy.

"Fuck everyone else," her daddy used to tell a young Katherine. "Everyone."

"Even you, daddy?" she'd ask.

Her old man smiled and took a sip of his coffee. "Especially me. If you can steal a penny from me without my knowing, I'll be so proud of you, Carmella. But if I catch you, I will break your fingers."

Katherine (who'd changed her name to Katherine with a long trail of forged documents lest anyone know who her father really was) had understood perfectly.

Be smart or be killed. So, whatever needed to be done. Make her daddy proud.

He sipped his coffee again but frowned when the bloody man on the floor started to moan. "You see this piece of shit? He's a mush. You know what a mush is, Carmella?"

She knew, but she didn't say anything. She liked hearing her daddy talk.

"I was winning the Boston College game. The spread was seven.

Up four with a minute to go. Then this mush walked into the room and I lost by a point. He's bad luck. Always has been. Even when we were kids. He did this to himself," her daddy said and put the coffee cup down on the table next to the handgun.

Little Carmella stared at the weapon. She'd seen plenty of them in every room of the house. She'd never touched one.

Her daddy held it up and smiled. "You think you're old enough to use this? You want to take care of this one for me? Huh?"

She didn't know if he was teasing or not. She hadn't made a move either way, just sitting with her hands folded on the table.

He handed her the weapon and she took it. Stood and walked around the table. The gun felt too heavy to lift, even with both hands.

"Here. Let me help you." Her daddy stood behind her, helping to raise the weapon high enough for her to use it. "It has a kick. It will probably knock you back. Don't be scared. I'm going to hold you, so you don't fall. You trust me?"

"Always." When the gun was settled, and she aimed at the man's head, she pulled the trigger. No hesitation. No regrets. No looking at the past.

Carmella fell back, but her daddy caught her in his arms. She pulled away and lifted the gun, aiming at his chest.

"Pull the fucking trigger or put it down already," he said. She remembered his eyes. No fear. Just pride.

She'd been unable to keep it raised and turned it over, handing it to her daddy. She'd sat back down and folded her hands, even when the men came to drag the lifeless body of her uncle away.

"You're going to do well, Carmella. Much better than your sister or your mother ever did." She had seen them both in pictures, but didn't know what had happened to them. Actually, she knew she'd always known the truth, but it was hard for an eight-year-old to come to terms with who her daddy was and what he was capable of.

She wondered now if he knew the full extent of what she'd accomplished in her life. She'd been eighteen when he'd been arrested for the last time. He had no chance of parole for all the slayings and the connections to The Family in New Jersey and a dozen other organizations he'd worked for over the years. Her daddy was a hitman-for-hire. He'd take everything he'd ever done to the electric chair if Vermont had their say.

Katherine was no longer Carmella. The media empire had always been under "another family name" even when it was side income. So, that's who she became and she made it into a real empire. She'd also been siphoning off hundreds of dollars from her daddy's bank accounts for months. Once he went to prison, she took it all. Cut the dead weight of her uncle that day and should have cut the dead weight of *Hidden Truth* a few months before all this started

Bought a building. A newspaper or four. Properties in six states. A bigger building than the original dump *Hidden Truth* stayed in. At one point, about ten years ago, she owned camels. She'd never actually seen them in person.

Katherine heard the machine gun firing inside the gas station. It was for the better because she was dwelling on a past she couldn't change and that had no bearing on her current situation.

While the driver kept pumping gas, his weapon in his free hand, the other one slipped around the vehicle and moved cautiously toward the front of the store. Armed men stepped out of the other vehicles, but stayed in position.

Katherine hoped this wasn't going to take long because she really needed to use the bathroom.

She stepped out of the vehicle.

"I think you'd be safer inside," the driver said.

"I don't pay you to think."

He shrugged. "Well, actually, that's exactly what you're paying me to do. If you're not safe, I don't get paid."

Where do men get their water, she thought. *From a fucking well, actually.*

Katherine smiled at the man. "Is that all I am? A paycheck?"

The man stared at Katherine. He wasn't smiling back. "As long as you pay me, you are safe. As long as you listen to my instructions, you'll stay alive and I'll get paid."

"Win-win," she said.

He nodded as the pump nozzle jumped, signaling the vehicle was full.

The man came out of the gas station, his weapon aimed at the sky. "All clear."

Katherine went to the front doors, the other man trailing behind her.

"It's all good. I had to kill a couple of guys standing around. I think they were robbing the place. The owner was already dead."

"I only care about the bathroom," Katherine said.

He held the door open for her. Such a gentleman.

As soon as she stepped inside, she smelled the foul odor of death.

Two men were on the floor in front of the counter, face-down and bloody.

Katherine went to the bathroom. The door was locked. She sighed. "I need the key."

One of the men got it for her and unlocked the bathroom. She couldn't remember which guy was which now. All three looked alike, with beady eyes and wearing all black.

"I'll be right here," he said.

"No, you won't. You're not listening to me piss. Find a plastic bag and fill it with potato chips. Nothing fancy, either. I don't like sour cream and onion flavored. No barbeque. Just original. And something to drink," she said.

"Like what?"

"Surprise me." She went into the bathroom and locked the door.

Katherine wondered where she was headed. Not in a metaphorical sense. In an actual *where the fuck are we going to drive to* sense. She had enough money to live a dozen lifetimes in comfort. It wasn't about the money. It never had been. It was always about the power it brought her and the motivation to do everything in her life she'd ever done.

She owned an island somewhere in the Bahamas. Near Johnny Depp's island, she thought she remembered. It would be easy enough to get on a boat and sail east. Call ahead and make sure the house was prepared. Katherine was sure she had a nice house there.

Then what? Get up at noon and watch the waves and stare at the sun when it went down at night? No thanks. She needed action. She needed someone to control. Maybe more than one person.

She could have all the money in the world, but if it didn't also mean power, it was worthless.

Katherine stared at herself in the gas station mirror and smiled. Despite her getting old, she was still a beauty. All without too much plastic surgery, either. At least she didn't think so.

When she exited the bathroom, her three bodyguards were watching the front of the building.

"Did you get me a drink?"

One of them nodded and held out a peach tea.

"Gross. I don't drink that garbage. Find me one with lemon. It has a leaf on the bottle." Katherine walked over to the two dead men on their bellies, with faces turned to the sides, toward each other. She was careful not to step in the pooling blood on the tile floor.

She pointed at the first one. He looked familiar. They both did. Could it really be them? "Turn these two over. I need a good look at their faces."

When all three men glanced at one another, Katherine repeated the order, only twice as loud.

The two men were flipped over, and she stared at their anguished faces.

"Do you know them, ma'am?"

Katherine couldn't stop looking at the two dead men.

"Here is a lemon tea with the leaf like you wanted."

Katherine put out her hand and took the bottle without taking her eyes off of the dead men.

"We have a car coming in hot," the bodyguard closest to the door said.

"Kill them if they stop," Katherine said and pulled her eyes away from the bodies.

For a second, when they'd both been flipped over, she'd thought they were Cull and Jackson.

Katherine was disturbed to realize, if it had been the two men, she would've been sad. It was an odd feeling.

She heard the vehicle as the driver slammed on the brakes and got out, a pretty redhead in magnificent red boots.

For fuck's sake …. Like a couple bad pennies ….

Her passenger was Steve, who didn't make as dramatic an exit from the car as his driver had.

Katherine went to the doors of the gas station and smiled. "Kill the man. I want to play with her before she dies."

CHAPTER 26

Howard Hughes Invented Death Ray That Can Kill Anyone on Earth

The red head reversed the car at high speed with the driver's door still open. Bullets rang off the engine metal and Anna braced for one to find its way through the dash into her gut. Steve curled into a ball on the seat and she couldn't tell if he was hit or not. Probably not used to this sort of thing, poor kid. He needed to get out more.

She took the street off the corner of the parking lot at full speed in reverse and barreled backward through the center turn lane of I-10. Maybe they were in Alabama. She had no idea, but she'd back all the way to Jacksonville again, if these psychos followed that far.

The windshield had washed white with damage around a dozen holes, but she wasn't looking that way anyhow. The glass came apart and poured in over her legs. She felt a cut, maybe a few, but she didn't look and didn't let off the gas. A hole punched through the back glass with jagged cracks out from it and all the way to the edge on every side. She could still see and still drove as the machine guns still fired. They must have been alternating reloading. They were trained to kill and apparently motivated to do it.

That botoxed, blond bitch had professionals? Why fire on me at a gas station then? Why the hell is she even here with them, if they're here to kill me? None of this shit makes sense.

Steve whimpered, so he wasn't dead, although this latest sad sack act was going to grow old fast, especially if they were fighting for their lives.

A blue compact swerved into the turn lane behind them. Anna steered left into the correct lane but going the wrong way. The blue piece of garbage swerved, too. She went back into the turn lane and it filled her path again. She went all the way over and the car did the same.

"Are you with them?" she asked the compact through the cracked back glass.

"She wants me dead. They're going to kill me."

"What're you talking about? What do you know about this?"

Steve stayed curled and didn't answer.

She realized the machine gun fire had stopped, but then it resumed. She decided to play the game of "chicken out." The mustang was toast anyway, and she thought she could rip through that pissy little blue car like crepe paper. If she turned just right at the last moment, the impact would turn the nose around and she could drive forward. The impact on the trunk wouldn't bother the engine. Old demolition derby trick. Although the engine probably leaked like an eighty-year-old's bladder from all the heavy weapons' fire at this point.

The blue car veered off into the ditch just in time to abort the collision.

"Jesus," Anna said, "I didn't know they made Mercedes that small."

The driver climbed out and swatted an airbag away as he stood on the street, staring at the retreating Mustang with his jaw unhinged. He still held his phone.

Anna made the turn anyway. She hit the gas and the brake at the same time. As the car spun, Steve unfolded himself and tried to watch the blurred world outside the remaining windows. The driver's door slammed shut. The car fishtailed as she shifted into a forward gear and raced east. She gained control and mostly held her lane.

As Steve stared backward, she waited for his head to explode. She couldn't hear the gunfire over the engine noise which sounded loud like usual, but out of tune like she had never allowed to happen before.

"What the hell is Marty doing in that ditch?"

She stared into the side mirror with wind blasting her in

the face from the missing glass. Her red hair whipped around her cheeks and back over the seat. The man from the tiniest Mercedes ever ran away from his wrecked car and into the woods.

Steve knew that dude? The attack from the station and this guy tailing, too? What the hell?

A line of four black SUV's raced behind them and kept pace. Two of the vehicles took over the other two lanes and formed a wall as they pursued. No gunfire yet, but they were closing. Anna squinted at Steve. "You think they're after you? Not me? What did you fucking do?"

"Stole money. A lot of it. All of it."

"From Carmella?"

"Who? No."

"Katherine Hemingway.... You stole her fucking money? That's rich. You're going to die, but that's rich, Brony Boy."

"Get me out of here and I'll cut you in. Half."

"Don't know if I can. In case you hadn't noticed from the fetal position, I've been trying."

"Sixty percent."

Anna laughed. "And here I thought my trip to Jacksonville had all been a waste. I am so glad I bagged you, Rainbow Dash. Wish you weren't getting me shot at, but still not my worst date so far."

They took to the air over the bridge and landed hard. A piece of metal bounced away from the car and over the side in a tight spin. After crossing the bridge, she turned hard and skid sideways before gaining traction. She raced up a service road and the SUVs fell into single file again to follow. They lost some ground, but started to catch up again.

Anna turned sharp onto a gravel road and bottomed out. Wasn't the first time in her life abusing her Mustang, but she thought that might be it for the muscle car. She held on though and spit gravel in every direction. The SUVs handled the terrain better than she'd hoped.

"They're gaining on us."

"Thanks for the update, Pinky Pie."

She ran hard onto another blacktop road and lost a lot of

speed. The front SUV caught the back fender and spun them. The rest pulled onto the road to block her in. Anna floored it and shot through a gap northbound. The SUVs were turned the wrong way and struggled to get out of each other's path as Anna left them behind on a wide curve.

"You did it."

"I sure as hell…."

Something snapped in the engine and the car whined high and shrill as the power went out of the Mustang. She jerked it into park and skidded sideways to block most of both lanes. "Get ready to run into the woods like your friend Marty back there."

A Chevy roared into view ahead of them and squealed to a stop with smoke boiling up behind the back wheels.

The men stepped out and Anna pulled the biggest silver handgun Steve had ever seen from under the seat. It had bright, red grips with silver snakes baring their fangs between her fingers and red nails.

Steve shook his head. "Fucking Jackson and Cull."

"Are they friends or with Carm…um, with Katherine?"

"They aren't with her." Steve eyed the gun. "You should still shoot them and then…ugh, we take their car."

"Good enough." She jumped out and pointed the gun at the sky in one hand instead of at them. "Give us a ride. Katherine is shooting at us."

"Who the hell are you?" Cull said.

Steve ran toward them. "I can't believe you guys are here. Did you fucking tell her where I was?"

"No, you told everyone where we were, so thanks for that, Dick," Cull said. "Marty told us where you were and wanted to form a Strange Bedfellows club."

"What?" Steve looked south past the dead Mustang and Anna's hand cannon. "We need to go now. They're coming."

"Just want to split the escape money, so we can all live free and into old age," Jackson said.

Anna pushed past Cull and climbed into the driver's seat. "Get in, if you want to live."

"Hey," Cull hopped in the back with Steve.

Jackson got back in the passenger's side as Anna backed away. He struggled to close his door and get on his seatbelt. She dropped the gun grip-up between her legs and her hiked dress. The SUVs rounded the curve at full speed. Anna spun the car and drove north again. The front SUV swerved around the Mustang on the right and barely held the shoulder. The second vehicle tried to plow through the muscle car, but crashed to a halt. The other two slowed enough to swerve around on both sides.

"She really wants you dead, Steve," Jackson said looking back.

"Who are you?" Cull shouted from the backseat.

Anna reached down between her legs and Jackson tensed as he thought she was going for the gun. She checked a couple scratches on her legs which matched her hair, nails, dress, and gun. Anna said, "She's been a cold, heartless killer since I was a kid. After my mother died, she wanted me to follow in her...."

"Who are you?!" Cull yelled louder and kicked the back of the driver's seat.

"You kick me again, you pruney Chucky Bukowski wannabe, and I'll open your third eye with a hollow point."

"How do you know Katherine Hemingway?" Jackson said.

"I'm her goddaughter...and her real sister's kid."

CHAPTER 27

Garden Gnomes Are Spies for the Upcoming Alien Invasion

Marty didn't need this shit. Any of it. He could be in the Bahamas by tomorrow. He'd find work. He always did. He didn't need a ton of money. A few bucks extra here and there to keep him entertained.

Maybe he could reinvent himself. Change his name. Dye his hair. He'd always wanted to be a blonde. One glance in the rearview mirror, and he knew he'd look ridiculous.

It doesn't matter anymore, he thought. *I could dye my hair like a fucking peacock and no one would pay any attention to me. I'd fit right in with the rest of the lunatics.*

The world had become a reimagining of *Mad Max*. Everyone in it was Mel Gibson, and not the loveable Mel from *Lethal Weapon*. This was the latter-day Gibson screaming profanity and anti-Semitic vitriol on taped phone calls.

He drove past two burning cars on the side of the road, as if God was telling Marty he was right about what was happening.

Someone stepped into the road, waving their arms, and Marty nearly overturned the vehicle, scratching the side of the car against the guardrail just getting it under control and stomping on the gas to get away before he was shot at.

It had taken him too long to get the car out of the ditch after the psycho gun parade had moved along. Another setup and he was done.

He refused to speak his plan out loud because it would sound even more ridiculous if he heard it.

You're going to follow and perhaps confront Katherine, he thought and pushed it back down, trying to bury it.

Why was he following instead of running? He wasn't a hero. Far from it. Marty had always been comfortable knowing he was a coward.

Marty was afraid, now that he'd set this insane plan of his into motion, he'd be unable to find Katherine. The Mustang nearly killing him had been a blessing in disguise, since his boss (former boss, he guessed) had been in pursuit. He recognized the Goon Squad black SUVs she always hired to protect her from phantom threats on her life.

Maybe they weren't so phantom in the grand scheme of things.

He needed to catch up to her convoy and figure out who was driving the Mustang and what part they had in all this.

He asked himself again why he was following Katherine instead of going in the opposite direction and washing his hands of the bitch. It would be so easy to start a new life. He knew he could work on what little conscience he had and slowly beat it down so he'd forget. Alcohol, maybe some coke, and definitely a hooker or two would ease himself into a better life.

A life without Katherine or *The Hidden Truth.*

All he had to do was take the next exit, turn around on the highway, and head away from all this.

On the road ahead would be more death and destruction. Someone had tried to run him off the road and take him out of the game permanently. Had it been a stranger? Marty's gut told him there was another player in this now.

Someone else way more dangerous than he was.

An exit came up, but Marty fought the urge to turn off and run, his tail between his legs.

I'm better than that, Marty lied to himself.

Despite wanting to act like the hero and finally getting to a place where he actually liked and respected himself, Marty was smart enough to know the real person he was could cut the wheel at any moment.

He stayed in the slow lane, closest to any upcoming exits.

He saw a car in the distance, well ahead of him, and in the opposite lane. He hadn't passed a car in miles.

The road ahead took him to...where? He didn't even know exactly where he was. Heading west? Maybe. It didn't matter in the grand scheme of things. Marty just felt like running until he ran out of gas or found a gas station still open without anyone trying to kill him. Same with food and lodging.

He didn't bother with the radio. It would either be filled with horrible news or, even worse, pre-recorded country music or religious talk. None of it was appealing.

A new game plan was in order. He couldn't drive forever. He needed to figure out where the safest place would be. Not in a big city. Probably not anywhere with a large population. He knew he was in the South, so everyone had a weapon on their person. Everyone who used to not carry was now armed and dangerous because of the app.

Not my fault. Well...not totally my fault, he thought. Cull and Jackson had opened up this rift to Hell. They'd invented this and tossed them all into chaos. It wasn't Marty's fault. He'd been as much a victim as everyone else trying to survive right now. He was nearly tortured to death and just avoided being raped by some monster. He'd kicked ass to get out of that, so maybe he could work something out here, too.

Marty slammed on the brakes just as he went past an exit and onto the overhead pass, unmindful if anyone was behind him. It didn't matter, anyway. He pulled up the ramp just far enough to see the action clearly. His focus was solely on the scene to his right, just off the exit ramp. He'd caught it briefly, but it took a second for his mind to register what he'd glimpsed.

The SUV's were fanned out in the parking lot of an abandoned fast food restaurant with matching goons in black suits and carrying machine guns moving in to surround the building. A vehicle, engine smoking and riddled with bullet holes, had crashed into the drive-thru sign.

Marty covered his mouth when he saw who was bursting from the side exit: Steve, Cull, Jackson, and a woman he didn't know.

They got about fifteen feet before the goons flanking from

both sides opened fire, chasing the group back inside the building.

Marty knew the smart move was to get the car moving and drive as far away as possible while they were all distracted.

He owed none of them anything. They'd conspired to ruin his life. Taken his steady income stream away. The potential to be super rich because of the *Hidden Truth* app, exposed some of his quirks and habits.

None of them deserved to live. The police weren't going to come to the rescue. No one was. The world was lawless and deadly right now.

Marty looked around. The highway was nearly empty, vehicles traveling it giving everyone else a wide berth. As cars crested the rise on the overpass they switched into the farthest lane, faces watching Marty as though waiting for him to open fire.

The world had gone mad.

Was he partially responsible? Could he take some of the blame?

Marty shook his head. *I was just doing my job. I had no idea any of this was going to happen. How could I know? She locked me out as soon as it was launched.*

Marty watched as the shooting began. He felt powerless to stop it. What was he supposed to do? He didn't have a weapon and even if he did, it wouldn't do any good. He was a lousy shot. He was too far away. The wind was blowing. And saving people wasn't in his varied but limited skillset.

A hundred other excuses flipped through his mind as he heard the shots and saw the armed men assaulting the building.

Marty turned away. He covered his ears, but he could still hear the gunfire.

He had a mental image of speeding up the ramp, around the service road, and plunging headfirst into battle. He'd run over a few of the fuckers before they could turn their guns on him. Maybe he'd clip Katherine, so she couldn't get away.

The men would turn in horror, guns raised, trying to shoot Marty, but he was in a car and he'd knock them down and run over their bodies, listening to them scream.

He'd circle the building, taking them all down.

Cull and Jackson would come running out with Steve and the mystery woman. Marty would wave them over, but at the last second, run them over, too.

Except for the woman. He'd hit her to stun, toss her and Katherine into the trunk of the car, and speed away.

He'd spend the next few weeks on his own Bahama island watching the two women do awesome lesbian stuff, just so he'd let them live.

Another gunshot rang out.

Marty ducked down in the car.

If he drove down there, they'd shoot him before he got into the parking lot.

Katherine would smile as bullets pierced his arms and chest. She'd make sure he lived, so she could torture him for days, in ways nipple-twisting Fat Manson could have never imagined.

Even if he managed to survive and capture Katherine, sooner or later, she'd escape. She was like a snake. A reptile. The woman was the fucking Devil.

No scenario ended well unless he drove away.

Marty sighed and fought back the tears. He was rattled. His nerves were shot.

Better than *being* shot.

He started the vehicle and forced himself to not look to the right, where he knew Cull, Jackson, Steve, and the woman were being killed at this very moment.

Marty Carroll, former editor of *The Hidden Truth*, decided to aim his car to the south and find a boat that would take him to an island getaway. It didn't matter where.

It didn't matter he was broke and would be out of gas soon.

None of this mattered anymore.

Marty turned on the radio and settled on a country music station to drown out the cowardly thoughts in his head.

CHAPTER 28

More Shocking Details about Fat Raymond's and Skinny Sylvester's Meth Empire Collapse.

Bullets tore through the walls of the restaurant which had been abandoned long before Cull and Jackson managed to fuck over the world and themselves with the *Hidden Truth* app. The place smelled like piss and cooked vomit as brick exploded in chunks through rotten paneling.

Steve turned over tables and then squatted down by a planter filled with pebbles and the brown dead corpses of ferns. Bullet fragments tore uneven holes through the sideways table tops as shrapnel bounced off.

Anna squared herself with her obscene red hand cannon gripped in a double fist. The last of the glass shattered out from the front windows and she turned from side to side seeking out a target. The men outside in suits which bulged out from body armor underneath ducked aside as they reloaded. Others stepped into the gap and opened up another expensive volley of aimless murder. Anna still twisted left and right looking for someone to shoot.

The planter, which Steve squatted in front of instead of behind for some reason, busted through with fist sized holes now that the walls and tables were Swiss cheese.

Cull and Jackson hit the floor, as the ordering counter took the brunt of the attack. Stray shots broke and rang through the metal edging off the counter.

Sheets of green plastic draped behind the counters, concealing the kitchen, and danced with the automatic fire which aimed high to clear the planter and counter.

Glass shattered in the foyer of the entrance to their left. A trash can cover blew apart in chunks of wood and plastic. The "Thank You" sign on the swing door for trash disposal broke in two and skidded across the floor. Bullets whizzed off the tile as a goon in sunglasses fired in on Jackson and Cull from the side.

Both men scrambled backward and prepared to dive over the counter. A stack of highchairs split down one side and tipped over onto the tile.

A man in goggles, a filter mask, a black apron, and acid wash jorts burst out from between the green plastic curtains. His big belly curved underneath the thick apron like a medicine ball and showed pale and hairy on both sides.

He leveled a shotgun at Cull and Jackson. They dropped to the floor instead of diving and they slid hard into the bullet-riddled side. Even though the machine gun to their flank still unloaded on them, Cull and Jackson stayed down on the exposed tile.

The Pot-Bellied Jort Monster fired. The shot struck the inside of the counter hard enough for them to feel it against their backs. None of it passed through except where a few pellets found escape through machine gun holes. Jackson took some in the back of his left bicep, but he didn't get up.

The gunman outside ejected and reloaded. Pot-Bellied Jort ratcheted and stepped up to the counter as if taking orders. He leaned out and fired onto the foyer entrance from directly over Cull's head. After that, both men heard an unrelenting, shrill ring in their ears which never fully let up. It seemed too far out of the effective range for a shotgun, but the gunman outside pitched backward and didn't rise.

The Jort Man ratcheted again and aimed straight down on Cull's crotch. Both men scramble to the sides as the tile in front of the counter obliterated under the shotgun's bore. Both men felt bee stings up and down the backs of their legs and ass, but they couldn't tell if it was pellet or tile shard.

The gun ratcheted a fourth time and Anna found her target. She blew a hole through the apron above where the broad belly met shriveled chest. Blood, bone, and organ erupted from Jort

Man's back out an exit wound a dozen times bigger than the crater between the hairy man-boobs. The ejecta splattered the green plastic in a gore-red Jackson Pollock Christmas mural. Jort Man made a dead-weight collapse to the floor with the authority of a meteorite.

The shotgun teetered on the edge of the counter and tilted over on the customer side. Cull caught it in the air and spun the stock to his shoulder. He swept the entrance, but no one stood there. Machinegun fire resumed from the front and further chewed apart the exterior.

Anna pulled Steve to his feet and hauled him around the planter by his arm.

Steve showed his teeth. "Fuck you two. You did this."

"You stole the money, genius," Jackson said. "Fuck yourself and enjoy being a multi-millionaire for the last minutes of your life."

Jackson and Cull hiked a leg each up onto the counter and swung their feet over as they felt the sting of the particles embedded in their ass cheeks.

Cull said, "Let's check his pockets for...."

A wiry stick figure of a man popped through the bloody plastic. He had on the goggles and a black apron like the Jort Corpse did, but was buck naked except for a forest green pair of Doc Martins with neon yellow laces.

He brandished an AR-15 with a homemade bump stock made of hardware store metal plates and screws locked around and through the trigger guard. "Fuck your fucking mothers, you motherfucking fuckers!"

Jackson and Cull rolled off the counter onto their faces on the ruined tile on the customer side. Naked Doc Martin fired, and the gun bounced in the bump at a near automatic rate. The AR kicked left, right, up, and down with the recoil firing. Naked Doc barely held on as he wasted eight shots on the floor and walls and then chewed apart the ceiling with the next twenty of the thirty rounds in the magazine.

Anna fired two shots as Steve pulled her off balance trying to run away sideways. She opened two large holes through one of the green plastic drapes. Metal impacts sounded behind the plastic sheets and someone screamed.

Naked Doc managed to level the AR-15 for the final two rounds. One went wild and sailed out through the empty front window. It took off the earlobe of one man who slapped the side of his head and bent over. It continued past Katherine Hemingway and missed her eye by two inches without her knowing. It crossed the highway and passed through the empty air where Marty's car had been moments before. It finally punched through a blue sign that warned people to buckle up because it was the law and deflected off the metal post into the dirt of the surface street shoulder.

The final round fired by Naked Doc tore into Steve's gut an inch above and to the right of his belly button at the same time that an M-16 round tore through the kidney on the other side. The bullets passed each other inside him and exited sloppy to go on their ways.

Steve stood on his toes and twisted out of Anna's grip. He fell to his side screaming and thrashed on the floor. His last complete sentence thought was that he wished he had called his mother and wished he'd given her some of the money before this happened. The rest of it was flashes of light and pain which eventually ended in a fiery heat his brain could not process.

Anna knelt over Steve and leveled her aim over the counter. Naked Doc ejected the empty magazine and reached for his boot. She fired through his balding scalp and caved in his skull. The bullet burrowed through his brain and through the center of this throat. It took out a lung, shattered bone, and turned guts into soup. It bounced, breaking hip bones before resting in the dead man's bowel. Naked Doc faceplanted on the floor with his knees bent and his bloody ass up in the air.

Jackson and Cull took to their feet and made to hurtle the counter.

Anna called, "Help me with Steve."

Jackson said, "Steve, is fucking...."

They dropped to the ground again, and a machine gun opened up through the drive thru window. Anna stood and stepped out to the side. She fired and turned the man's head into a canoe.

Katherine yelled from outside, "Hold your fire! Whoever is still alive in there...."

Jackson's and Cull's ears rang too much for them to hear it. They finally made it over the counter. Cull searched the dead man's jorts and filled his own pockets with the red shot shells.

Jackson turned his head away from all of Naked Doc's leaking holes. He braced his feet against the body of the AR-15 and wrestled the shoddy bump stock loose.

"Help me with Steve!"

Neither Jackson nor Cull responded. Katherine continued jawing outside.

Cull pulled two complete magazines out of Naked Doc's boots. He handed them to Jackson and then Jackson recharged the weapon. Cull pulled a sheath and hunting knife out of a boot and kept that for himself.

Someone behind the plastic shouted, "Stop fucking around. Get down the tunnel."

They heard that.

Anna was screaming about something behind them.

"Leave him," Jackson said. "They have an escape tunnel."

Cull and Jackson exchanged a look as they crouched. They swept aside the curtains as a man in goggles disappeared down a trap door and closed it over him. It looked just like the tile, and they would have never found it, if they hadn't seen it.

The kitchen had been renovated and had working florescent lights overhead. Tanks, tubing, trays, and white crystals filled the room. Chemicals burned Jackson's and Cull's eyes and throats.

"Fucking meth cooks," Cull said and coughed.

"Let's get that...." Jackson never finished.

Flame swept over the surface of the tables along the walls from one of the ruptured tanks. The fire ringed the room and then climbed up the other tanks. Something popped and hissed and then a second tank was spraying like a flamethrower. The heat became everything, and their view of the world rippled. Fire washed over the ceiling with an inverted tide rising out of Hell.

Jackson and Cull sprinted out of the fast food kitchen meth

lab and dove over the counter in the air. Anna covered Steve with her body, but he still felt all the heat from the explosion without understanding it.

Jackson thought he heard Katherine's voice call his name for a second.

The back of the building vanished, and the front of the restaurant folded away from itself.

CHAPTER 29

As the World Rebuilds from the Hidden Truth Reign of Terror: Where Are the Key Players Now?!

She watched What's His Name with the weird mustache stagger backward from the drive thru window and spill his brains to fertilize the weeds growing through the parking lot. Somehow that awful mustache survived the total destruction of his face. Such a shame that.

Katherine yelled, "Hold your fire!"

Her men obeyed quicker than she expected. It surprised her, and she had to think for a second of what to say next. They were all still training their aim and attention at the building or what was left of it. Whole thing seemed ready to blow right over.

"…whoever is still alive in there…"

What the fuck do I intend to say next? Still alive in there?! Hey, no hard feelings. We mean you no harm…

Someone was still alive. They shot What's His Name above his shitty mustache.

Had to be that fucking bitch niece with her stupid ass gun. She might have to lose a few more guys to drag her out, but it….

"Help me with Steve!"

Oh, fucking perfect. Her and Steve. Maybe enough time to twist the truth out of Steve before he bleeds out. What a fucking day.

"Anne Marie, put down your gun and let us in. We'll bring him and you out. You have my word."

"Fuck you. I'll cave in your plastic face with a hollow point, you crusty cunt!"

Katherine clicked her tongue and shook her head. The whole "you have my word" was a real overplay. She knew it was a mistake as soon as she said it.

"Listen, I'm sorry about what happened to your mother. We never got along, but I never intended it to go…"

"You're a killer and a soulless twat. One of us is dying today, and I got no plans on it being me."

Another voice. Male. She couldn't make out what they shouted over the top of Anne Marie's insults and threats. Might be Jackson or Cull. One or both of them might still be alive.

Katherine felt a thrill inside her, but didn't understand why.

"Talk some sense into her, guys. She's about to get both of you killed. Let's walk away from this a little richer and still alive."

Her again. "Go to Hell you shriveled up piece of…."

Katherine didn't wait for the Bitch in Red to finish this time. "Jackson? Cull? This doesn't have to end with everyone…."

The explosion was so intense and exaggerated that Katherine saw it happen clearly and did not believe it was real in the same instant. The heat overwhelmed her and blurred her eyes with a wash of defensive tears.

The back of the building became a sunburst which reversed the shadows from the weaker ball of fire in the sky. Brick and metal blasted off for orbit, but then were consumed in flashfire before it could return to Earth.

The front of the building peeled away from itself and then she was airborne and flying backward on a wall of heat. Somehow, she hit two different SUVs before she bounced along the ground.

She couldn't figure it out, even after days in a private hospital or the weeks of recovery in a French villa, after that. She still had security forces, but never any of the guys from that day. She wasn't even sure if any of them survived around that crater which opened up into Hell. They were wearing armor and she wasn't, but she survived. She was richer, stronger, and more deserving, so who knew?

She never bothered to ask about those hired guns, but she did have people looking for Jackson and Cull. Deep down she knew they could have never survived, but part of her damaged head wouldn't let her let it go.

So, she didn't try to resist the urge.

CHAPTER 30

Katherine Hemingway Still Hides in Swiss Bunker Avoiding Seal Team 6

Jackson, Cull, and Anna emerged from the dry sewer tunnel where it opened into a stagnant cesspool. Smoke and dust drifted past them and escaped the opening. Jackson felt like he had fallen forever before they regrouped in the tunnel. He was surprised not to be dead as fire still erupted from where the drive thru meth lab had been. He was simply shocked to be alive and moving, although he started to feel every joint and burn now. He kept checking his scorched clothes to be sure he wasn't still on fire.

He returned his attention to the AR-15 in his hands as Cull scanned outside with the shotgun ready.

"Let's keep moving," Anna said behind them. Her dress was smeared with soot and dust. Her hair was salted with concrete chips. But she looked ten times better off than the two of them.

"Do you think those assholes are out here waiting for us?" Jackson said.

"Which assholes?" Anna said. "The ones with Carmella or the ones whose meth lab we just blew up."

Jackson said, "I don't want to mix it up with either one before I pick all the shrapnel out of my ass."

Cull said, "The tweekers are running for the hills. Katherine has to think we're dead, but I don't want to hang around until she stumbles on us again."

They worked their way around the edge of the cesspool. Jackson's left shoe slipped in and he felt the filth ooze between his toes. He still smelled it on himself as they limped north away from the tunnel.

Jackson spit grit out from between his teeth. "I can't believe we found Steve and then didn't get the bank account info from him."

"You could have helped me keep him alive long to get it out of him," Anna said.

"Shit." Jackson shook his head. "I thought you were doing that because you cared about him."

"I'd given up on Carmella's bullshit and just picked him up for fun, but then when it turned out he was the reason…. Fuck it. Doesn't make any difference now."

Cull said, "You were pissed at me for siphoning that money from Marty's stash to begin with, and now that it's gone, you miss it."

"I still blame you for all of this, Cull."

"I knew it! Yeah, sorry I fucked up your beautiful apocalypse, Mr. Wrath."

The railyard came into view ahead of them between the trees. As they approached the detached cars on the tracks, gunfire popped off behind them. Shots sparked off the metal of the cargo cars.

They found it in them to run. They crouched behind the wheels inside the yard as more bullets rang off the tracks on both sides of them.

"It's not automatic weapons," Cull said.

"The tweekers are drawing down on us?" Jackson said. "Why? Those guys built an escape tunnel. Why aren't they just escaping?"

"We blew up their shit, I guess." Cull stuck his head out far enough to peep with one eye as the gunfire petered off. "They're coming. Still in those crazy ass aprons. Who are these fuckers?"

Jackson stood. "Let's go."

As they ran from the train cars, more shots rang out and shouts rose behind them.

"All of this bullshit is going to alert Carmella's thugs of where we are," Anna said.

"Us being dead will quiet things down," Jackson said. "Just keep running."

They stopped and put their backs to the side of a warehouse. A single blue convertible sat in the parking lot three hundred feet away.

Cull pointed with the shotgun. "What do you think are the odds the keys are inside?"

Anna said, "I can hotwire it, if we need to."

"I can, too," Cull said, "but I don't have the tools on me and we don't have the time if we're running out into the open under fire to do it."

"I guess I'm just better than you," she said.

Jackson leaned out from the wall, and a bullet burrowed through the gravel a couple feet out from his toes.

"We need breathing room either way." Cull held the shotgun out sideways without looking. Jackson plugged his ears with his fingers and Cull blasted off a shot. The sound roared through the yard. The men in aprons screamed and scattered. He pulled back to cover and worked the action to prepare another shell.

Jackson leaned out and fired off a few rounds at the men scattering for cover. His third shot caught one man in the thigh through his apron. The dude tumbled to the ground behind a rock pile.

Jackson stopped firing as he watched the fattest woman he had seen in a long time running naked except for an apron she couldn't possibly tie in the back and a pair of flip flops. She moved fast for all her hinderances. A tramp stamp of a heart with angel wings jiggled above her monstrous bare ass. If he fired, he couldn't have missed, but he just stared in wonder.

Return fire peppered the warehouse and he pulled back against their cover. "Do we stay put, go for the car, or what?"

The blue convertible started and peeled out of the parking lot backward. Anna made a hard turn and drove forward along the two-lane road away from the black smoke rising from the meth lab in the distance.

"That bitch," Cull said.

"Let's go."

They ran along the side of the warehouse toward the road.

A guy in goggles, black jeans, and a Slayer tee shirt jumped out in front of them. He fired a .45 and the bullet skimmed along the metal wall above their heads. Cull fired back and ratcheted again before the headless body hit the ground.

Jackson made the corner of the building and fired off a few rounds. Cull grabbed up the .45 from the dead tweeker's hand, and they made a run for it.

CHAPTER 31

Indian Casinos May Be a Front for Mafia, White Slavery, and Alien Experimentation on Conservative Christians.

Cull pushed the carton for the frozen dinner toward the center of the table which was the same color wood as the walls of the cabin. Then, he stood up. Alfredo sauce ran down the side onto the wood.

"I'm going to pop into the casino tonight."

Jackson looked up from a worn paperback of Jack Ketchum's *Off Season*. "Going to change it up, huh?"

Cull stuck up a middle finger as he stretched. "You feeling neglected, honey?"

"I feel you're going to get seen in a building full of cameras and someone will track us down before we can get out."

"It's an Indian casino and we're out in the woods. They aren't sharing tape with white dudes, I'm sure."

Jackson went back to his book. "I'm not sure. Feds are trying to track down everyone from *Hidden Truth* and God knows what Katherine might be doing. We can lay low, get everything we need delivered, keep working online scam money, and figure out a real plan before we get seen."

"You go down to that used bookstore all the time. They know your alias like you're old friends."

"Yeah, I'm sure they have the used bookstore staked out. Just don't get us caught before I figure this all out."

"Yes, dear." Cull moved toward the door. "You can keep the papers for the car, so I don't gamble it away."

"You going to throw your dinner away?"

"I'll get it when I get back."

"What does that even mean? You have to pass the trashcan to get to the door."

"I don't want to lift anything right after I eat."

Cull left Jackson reading and hiked down the hill toward the outskirts of town which hung along a single road on the side of a mountain. He could have thrown the carton away, but it bothered Jackson, and Cull just couldn't bring himself not to fuck with the guy a little every day.

He walked along the road past the gift shops and nodded at the tourists. Part of him wondered if any of them might recognize him from the old app. He passed the casino and kept going. Cull walked up to a Motor Inn and then through a corridor to a trailer out back

Cull knocked. The door opened, and he stepped inside. The kid pushed his glasses up on his nose and closed the door. He sat back down at his computer without saying anything. The place smelled like feet and old chili.

"Wouldn't kill you to clean up a little," Cull said.

"Wouldn't kill you to mind your own fucking business either."

"Maybe." Cull shrugged. "Doesn't usually pay as well. Speaking of paid…."

"Still working. Found all the accounts, but it's a banking firewall. It'd be easier to hack some governments."

"How much longer?"

"I don't…. What the hell?"

Cull leaned over the kid's back. "What is it?"

"We got found out. They're in my system."

"The bank?"

"No, this is like a ransomware. They're in."

"Can you turn it off?"

"They'll still have control." The kid tapped the keys. "We might have to pay to get control back."

"How much?"

Before the kid could answer, a black rectangle popped up on the screen. Green letters typed out: GOOD TO SEE YOU ARE STILL ALIVE AND WELL, MR. STAPLES.

"Who the hell is, Mr. Staples?"

"Who is this? Can you tell?"

"No."

A green cursor flashed under the message.

"Can we type something back?"

"I guess."

Cull pushed the kid aside in his chair and leaned over the keyboard to peck with one finger: WHO IS THIS?

Cull hit enter and waited a couple seconds.

YOUR LADY IN RED. SORRY TO LEAVE YOU IN A LURCH. GIRL'S GOT TO TAKE CARE OF HERSELF IN THIS CRAZY WORLD.

"Fucking Anna."

"Who is this?" The kid got out of his chair and backed away. "What have you got me into?"

"I said it's Fucking Anna. Now shut up. You knew we've been trying to rob a fucking bank for weeks. Don't act like you're clean and dumb as driven snow now."

WHAT DO YOU WANT?

The person on the other end, presumably Anna, responded: SAME THING YOU DO. STEVIE'S STASH AND TO KEEP FROM GETTING CAUGHT BY AUNTIE. SHE'S STILL LOOKING FOR YOU TWO, BTW.

"What does 'BTW' mean?" Cull asked.

"It means 'By The Way'.... How fucking old are you?"

Cull had to backspace several times to get his next line typed: LISTEN. WE'RE NOT INTERESTED IN TROUBLE.

LIKE HELL, she typed. YOU CAN'T DO ANYTHING ELSE. WE NEED TO JOIN UP AND POOL RESOURCES. THERE ARE OTHER PEOPLE LOOKING FOR STEVIE'S TREASURE. NONE OF THEM ARE AS FAR AS YOU AND ME. WE ARE GETTING IN EACH OTHER'S WAY THOUGH. TIME TO TEAM UP FOR OUR COMMON GOOD. I KNOW WHERE YOU ARE. I'LL CALL AT THE CABIN IN A COUPLE DAYS.

Cull started to type again, but the rectangle vanished, and the computer unlocked.

"What's happening?" the kid asked. "Are we getting busted?"

"No, you're fine. Our operation is just expanding, I guess. I just have to have another uncomfortable conversation with an old friend."

Cull left the trailer and followed the road back toward the cabin. This time he did stop at the casino. He ordered his first two drinks before he placed his first bet.

ABOUT THE AUTHORS

Armand Rosamilia is a New Jersey boy currently living in sunny Florida, where he writes when he's not sleeping. He's happily married to a woman who helps his career and is supportive, which is all he ever wanted in life...

He's written over 150 stories that are currently available, including horror, zombies, contemporary fiction, thrillers and more. His goal is to write a good story and not worry about genre labels.

He not only runs two successful podcasts: **Arm Cast: Dead Sexy Horror Podcast**—interviewing fellow authors as well as filmmakers, musicians, etc. & **The Mando Method Podcast** with co-host Chuck Buda—talking about writing and publishing, but he owns the network, Project Entertainment Network, that produces them!

He also loves to talk in third person... because he's really that cool.

You can find him at http://armandrosamilia.com for not only his latest releases but interviews and guest posts with other authors he likes! You can also e-mail him to talk about zombies, baseball and Metal: armandrosamilia@gmail.com

Jay Wilburn is a Splatterpunk Award-nominated author with work in *Best Horror of the Year* Volume 5. He recently survived a kidney transplant and is currently training for a double marathon. His work includes the novel *Vampire Christ, Yard Full of Bones*, the nonfiction work *How to Make No Friends Everywhere*, and the children's series The Lake Scatter Wood Tales. He is the 2019 winner of the KillerCon Gross Out Contest. Check him out at JayWilburn.com, @AmongTheZombies on Twitter and Instagram, or on his Patreon page patreon.com/JayWilburn

Curious about other Crossroad Press books?
Stop by our site:
http://store.crossroadpress.com
We offer quality writing
in digital, audio, and print formats.